CHESS NUTS

*'Don't go too fast,' Jackson called
as he ran past Anna.*

*'You can only go so fast because there's nothing
between your ears!' Anna yelled back.*

Jackson is sporty and popular.

He's not the type to join the chess squad,
and Anna doesn't want him there.

But the game is set to change.

PUFFIN BOOKS

Published by the Penguin Group
Penguin Group (Australia)
250 Camberwell Road, Camberwell, Victoria 3124, Australia
(a division of Pearson Australia Group Pty Ltd)
Penguin Group (USA) Inc.
375 Hudson Street, New York, New York 10014, USA
Penguin Group (Canada)
90 Eglinton Avenue East, Suite 700, Toronto, Canada ON M4P 2Y3
(a division of Pearson Penguin Canada Inc.)
Penguin Books Ltd
80 Strand, London WC2R 0RL England
Penguin Ireland
25 St Stephen's Green, Dublin 2, Ireland
(a division of Penguin Books Ltd)
Penguin Books India Pvt Ltd
11 Community Centre, Panchsheel Park, New Delhi – 110 017, India
Penguin Group (NZ)
67 Apollo Drive, Rosedale, North Shore 0632, New Zealand
(a division of Pearson New Zealand Ltd)
Penguin Books (South Africa) (Pty) Ltd
24 Sturdee Avenue, Rosebank, Johannesburg 2196, South Africa

Penguin Books Ltd, Registered Offices: 80 Strand, London, WC2R 0RL, England

First published by Penguin Group (Australia), 2010

10 9 8 7 6 5 4 3 2

Text copyright © Julia Lawrinson 2010

The moral right of the author has been asserted.

Cover and text design by Allison Colpoys © Penguin Group (Australia)
Cover and internal illustrations by Allison Colpoys
Typeset in Janson Text 12.5/19pt by Sunset Digital Pty Ltd, Brisbane, Queensland
Printed and bound in Australia by McPherson's Printing Group, Maryborough, Victoria

National Library of Australia
Cataloguing-in-Publication data:

Lawrinson, Julia.

Chess nuts / Julia Lawrinson.

ISBN 978 0 14 330470 8 (pbk.)

Friendship in children – Juvenile fiction.

A823.4

puffin.com.au

Julia Lawrinson

CHESS NUTS

PUFFIN BOOKS

To Andrew Forbes-Macphail
Chess Nut extraordinaire

John Farrell
Chess Coach extraordinaire

And Rob and Enno
My worthy opponents

Chess is everything: art, science and sport.
Anatoly Karpov

Jackson was running.

It was his third time around, and he could hear the voices at the finish line, cheering and calling.

'Jackson, Jackson.'

Jackson didn't have to look to know how far ahead of Flash Buckley he was – he felt the blood and breath rushing in his ears and the soar between each step, and he knew.

Flash was fast, and plenty of times they had been neck-and-neck in a race, but Jackson had always managed to edge Flash out. If Jackson won the cross-country today, he'd be one step closer to Outstanding Athlete of the Year for the third time in a row. And it really mattered, because it was their last year of primary school. Flash wouldn't get another chance.

'Jackson! Jackson!'

They were chanting for him, like they did in soccer, when he was running down the flank, or in cricket, when he leapt towards a ball that nobody thought he could catch, or hit the winning six for their side.

'Jackson, Jackson.'

The finishing line was in sight. All the kids in his house were going mad, and even some of the kids in the other houses were barracking for him.

He slowed down.

'Come on, Jackson! Come on!'

Jackson shrugged, and kept up the jog.

He was fifty paces from the line when he looked around. It took him a startled moment to realise that Flash was right there, approaching fast, his face puffed and red and angry.

In a blink, Jackson sprang from jogging to sprinting, almost losing balance as he did. Flash was in his ear now, breathing harsh and hard. It sounded like he was saying, 'Gotcha, gotcha,' and then they were running, their legs moving at the exact same time, feet thumping the ground. Jackson ran harder than ever before, but he could see Flash's feet stretching in front of his.

Right, Jackson thought.

He found strength he didn't know he had; he willed himself to go even faster, to hit the ground hard and push it away harder.

When he crossed the line, the crowd exploded. Jackson stopped and leaned his hands on his knees to catch his breath. Once he'd straightened up he looked around at all the kids from all the houses waving their flags, yelling words he didn't understand.

He couldn't work out whether he'd won or lost. Flash Buckley was sitting on the ground, his head between his knees, shoulders heaving. Chelsea T, who came in after them, looked like she'd got her breath back already.

Ms S, the head of sports, approached them and said, 'We'll wait for everyone to finish, and then we'll announce the winner and the runners-up.'

'He won, didn't he?' Jackson said, nodding towards Flash, who was getting to his feet.

'As I said,' Ms S looked from Jackson to Flash and back again, 'we'll make the announcement soon. You three go up to the podium when you're ready.'

Oh great, Jackson thought. With all the little kids who were racing, that was going to take forever.

There was a commotion among the spectators.

'Jackson!' yelled Jackson's house, Macquarie.

'Flash Buckley!' yelled Flash's house, Cook.

'Jackson!'

'Flash Buckley!'

The chants between the houses were getting louder and louder. Obviously nobody could tell who had won.

Jackson watched the other kids staggering over the finish line. The faster kids had already come in, and now there was a parade of young kids, kids who liked running but couldn't hack long distance, and kids who'd run because they'd been made to.

A group of year six girls came up and said, 'So, Jackson, did you win?'

Jackson shrugged. 'Dunno.'

'We hope you did,' one of them said.

'Yeah,' another added. 'We want you to beat Flash.'

'We'll see.'

'Bye, Jackson!' they said, and then walked over to their houses, giggling.

The very last person to finish was Anna. Anna was a chess geek, and she must have been forced to race, because her face was sulkier than it normally was, and she hadn't run a step. On his last lap, Jackson had called over his shoulder, 'Don't go too fast!' as a joke, but Anna had taken offence and yelled one of her insults back at him. He felt bad, because he secretly liked the way Anna didn't care less about anything. Even when the whole school made noises at her when she crossed the line, she ignored them.

Finally, over the PA, Jackson heard Ms S say, 'And now, Phoenix School, the result you've been waiting for. Cook, can you hear me?'

The kids from the blue house waved and cheered.

Then Ms S yelled, 'And what about you, Macquarie?'

The yellow house yelled even louder than Cook.

'It gives me great delight to announce the winner of the cross-country.'

The entire school went quiet. Jackson could feel everyone's eyes on him.

Come on, Jackson thought. Put me out of my misery.

'It's a tie between Jackson and Flash Buckley!'

Every kid in the school started yelling then, some in indignation, some in delight. Cook and Macquarie started up their victory chants.

Jackson was relieved, but only for a second. He could have won. Easy. But he hadn't.

Ms S announced that Chelsea had come third, and congratulated everyone who took part. Then she told everyone to collect their rubbish, go to the undercover area, and wait for the final siren.

Flash Buckley came up and shook Jackson's hand like he wanted to break it.

'What sort of a race was that?' He scowled.

'You almost won.'

'You almost let me.'

Jackson shrugged.

'What'd you pike for?'

'Dunno.'

'Next time,' Flash growled, 'you're road kill.'

'As if,' Jackson said.

Ms S cleared her throat, and Flash and Jackson stopped talking.

'Well, boys,' she said, 'this has never happened before. But I suppose as long as there's not a draw for the swimming, we'll still be able to have a clear result.'

'What about another race?' Flash said, looking sideways at Jackson.

Ms S raised her eyebrows. 'I don't think that'll be necessary, Mr Buckley. Anyway, well done to both of you for today.'

Flash gave Jackson one last glare, then went off with Adam and Ben. Ben slapped Flash's shoulder, and then ran a few staggering steps with his hands flapping and his knees knocking together. Jackson knew they were mocking him, and he wanted to go and whack Ben, but Ms S was still standing there.

'What happened, Jackson?' Ms S said. 'You'd just about won.'

Jackson looked away and mumbled, 'Dunno, miss.'

She sighed. 'Oh well. I'm sure you did your best. See you tomorrow.'

Jackson waited until she'd jogged back towards the undercover area before he turned and ran home.

'Shhh,' his mother said as he came in. 'Your father's sleeping.'

Jackson shrugged. His father was always sleeping these days.

'How'd you go?'

'I drew,' Jackson said, 'with Flash Buckley.'

'Flash?' said his mother. 'I thought you could beat him any day of the week. That's what you said this morning.'

'I know,' Jackson said. 'I just . . . didn't.'

'Do you want something to eat? Your father's lunch is there, if you want it.'

'I don't want anything,' Jackson snapped, and headed for his room.

'There's no need to be rude,' his mother hissed, trying to keep her voice low. Jackson closed the door to his room. He wanted to slam it, but he didn't dare wake his dad.

He sat on his bed, going over the end of the race in his head. He thought about it until he felt like his brain was going to burst.

Then, when he got sick of thinking, he pulled his Nintendo DS out of its case, turned it on, and started a game of chess.

'Don't go too fast,' Jackson called as he ran past Anna.

'You can only go so fast because there's nothing between your ears!' Anna yelled back. She was so angry she found herself walking faster for a moment.

Jackson wasn't the only one who'd overtaken her, or made comments. Not that Anna cared. She was only doing the cross-country because Ms S had made her.

'Come on, Anna,' Ms S had started off saying. 'At least give it a go.'

But Anna wouldn't. Ms S offered this and that, but finally she got hardline and said, 'If you don't participate, I'm going to have a word to

Mr F about whether you can take part in the Chess Championships.'

Bang.

Cross-country it was.

Cross-country was a dumb name for it, as far as Anna was concerned – it wasn't cross-anything, except the teachers' car park, the parents' car park, the outside of the junior and senior ovals, and then through a thicket of trees that lined the perimeter of the school's south side. Why would anyone want to run around that, especially in the freezing winter air? Why would anyone want to run, full stop? Last time she ran, in the D-grade netball competition, Flash Buckley had called her a retard. A teacher overheard him, and he got kept after school, plus he had to apologise to Anna in front of the class. She'd decided then and there she was never going to run in front of anyone at school again. Ever.

So Anna decided that if she had to do cross-country, she would do it, all right – walking all the way.

'Pick up the pace, Anna!' Ms S called as Anna sauntered by.

'Sure, miss,' Anna waved. She walked a bit faster, but as soon as she was out of Ms S's sight, she slowed down again.

Anna felt a whoosh of cold air by her ear. It was Flash Buckley, trying to cut corners as much as he could to catch up with Jackson. Anna was walking as close to the witches' hats as she could without being illegal, but Flash had ducked inside her.

'Idiot!' Anna called after him.

'What's the matter, super-brain?' Flash yelled back. 'Afraid you might lose a brain cell if you run? Ha ha.'

'Jackson was here five minutes ago, you troglodyte,' Anna bellowed. 'You've got no chance!'

The number of kids on the course dwindled. Finally, the slowest of the little kids ran past her. She was alone. Last. It meant that the whole school was waiting for her. Anna knew what was going to happen, and it wasn't going to be nice.

Ms S came jogging over as Anna was on the home stretch.

'Come on, Anna,' she said. 'We can't make the announcement until you get there.'

'Why can't you do it without me?' Anna said, slowing down even more.

'Because it's a school event,' Ms S said. 'And you're part of the school. I don't need to explain that to you, do I?'

Anna was tempted to start running, to make the end come faster. But there was no way. Even though what ended up happening was just as humiliating.

As soon as they saw her, they started calling and shouting.

'Boo!' called some.

'Come on!' called others.

Anna tried to keep her face perfectly still. It was so unfair. She hadn't wanted to do the cross-country in the first place, so why should they yell at her? Out of the corner of her eye she saw Flash Buckley, Jackson and Chelsea near the podium, waiting for their moment of glory.

Anna hated them all.

Once she'd finally made it to the finish line, she marched to the back of her house, scowling. Masha shot her a sympathetic look from where she was sitting reading her book while the rest of her house were cheering. Anna shrugged and looked away. The rest of the school didn't have to turn out to watch the Chess Championships, even though chess was a million times more interesting than cross-country. Why should she have to put up with this?

But even Anna was surprised when she heard Ms S say, 'It's a tie between Jackson and Flash Buckley!'

Maybe Jackson had tripped, or something. How else could Flash have managed to catch up with him?

But she didn't think about it long. The minute the other kids started moving towards the under-cover area, Anna turned around and stomped away in the opposite direction. She didn't care about her bag. She didn't care about anything. When she was outside the view of the school, she took off as fast as she could without actually running, and didn't stop until she reached home.

The classroom was almost silent, even though it was lunchtime, and even though it was full of kids. Normally the only time a room was quiet was when it had no kids in it, but C4 wasn't just a classroom. It was also Phoenix School's chess room.

At lunchtime, all the chairs were moved around and the desks separated so that each desk could fit two players. From Monday to Wednesday anyone could come to learn chess, but on Thursday and Friday only squad members were allowed to play. People could watch if they wanted to, but they had to be quiet.

'"Strategy requires thought, and tactics require observation",' Mr F said. 'Who said that, team?'

'Don't know, sir,' the kids replied.

'Grandmaster Max Euwe said that,' Mr F said. 'Remember that – thought and observation. And what do thought and observation require?'

'Don't know, sir.'

'Silence!' Mr F said, banging his fist down on the nearest desk so that half the pieces fell over. 'What's the golden rule of chess, team?'

'Silence!'

'Exactly.' Mr F beamed.

But today, it wasn't silent. Almost, but not quite.

The kids looked up from their games, and over at Josh. Josh was in the special education class. He had glasses that were always smudged, and when he talked, which wasn't often, he talked very slowly, as if his mouth didn't work properly. But one Thursday lunchtime earlier in the year, Josh had walked into the chess room. Nobody paid him much attention – the A- and B-teams were practising their openings. The number one of the B-team, Elias, was about to challenge Anna, the number one of the A-team, when

Josh plonked himself down at the table across from Elias.

'Josh,' Elias said, 'you're not in squad. You have to wait until Monday.'

But Josh didn't move. He didn't look Elias in the face, but he took a white pawn and a black pawn, hid them in his palms, then held out his fists so Elias could pick one.

'Go away,' Elias said. 'We're practising. You're not.'

But Josh didn't leave the table. He kept his head down and shook his fists at Elias. Mr F came along and said, 'What's going on?'

'Josh won't get up,' Elias complained. 'Get him to go away, Mr F.'

Mr F squatted down next to Josh. 'You want to play, do you?'

Josh nodded. Mr F nodded back. He was used to kids saying they could play, but they didn't know how to move a knight, or how to take a piece, or even that white moved first.

Elias waited for Mr F to tell Josh to leave. Mr F took squad just about as seriously as the players did, and he wasn't going to let Elias waste his lunchtime playing with a special ed kid, not when the finals were so close.

But instead of saying, 'Josh, come back on Monday with the others,' Mr F stood up and said, 'Elias, pick a hand.'

'What?' Elias said. 'You can't be serious.'

'I'm serious,' Mr F said.

'But, sir – '

' "Chess is a sea in which a gnat may drink and an elephant may bathe." Who said that?'

'Don't know, sir,' Elias said.

'Neither do I,' Mr F said. 'It's a Hindu proverb.'

'But, sir – '

'Silence. Begin.'

Elias sighed really loudly, in case Mr F hadn't noticed how irritated he was. Anna sat down to watch, and folded her arms. Anna and Elias looked at each other, and their look said, *Can you believe this?* A couple of spectators drifted by, and stayed.

Elias flicked his fingers at one of Josh's fists. Josh uncurled his hand: it was black. That meant that Josh was white, and went first.

Everyone waited for Josh to move a white pawn in a diagonal, or move a bishop as if it was checkers, or do something equally stupid, but Josh moved his king's pawn two spaces, which was a pretty common beginning. Elias frowned, and moved his black pawn up to the centre too. Josh placed another pawn up next to the first on the king's side.

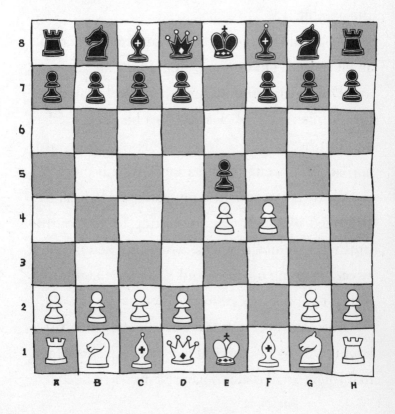

Elias frowned even more – it looked as if Josh was deliberately opening with the King's Gambit, which was not something Elias would have expected Josh to know. Elias had a choice now: either he took the new pawn and waited to see how Josh would respond, or else he could leave it there, and move his dark-squared bishop up and put pressure on Josh's knight. Elias decided he would accept the gambit.

Josh didn't seem to be paying much attention as he played. He swung on his chair, he hummed something that sounded like a funeral march, he picked his nose and wiped it on his shorts. Elias was surprised when Josh moved his knight forward, and so Elias went on the attack and advanced his rook's pawn to try to mess up Josh's pawn structure. It looked like Josh was attempting to get control of the centre of the board, which is essential for a strong opening in chess, and Elias was determined not to let it happen.

But with every attack Elias made, Josh had a counter-attack. Elias couldn't work out how Josh managed to make such smart moves when he didn't even seem to be watching the board.

Elias was planning an attack on Josh's queenside, and concentrating so hard that he didn't notice that Josh was planning an attack of his own. When Josh got behind Elias's defences and pinned his king and queen with a knight, Elias laid his king down, pushed his chair backwards, and stormed out of the room.

'Wow,' said Anna.

'Hmmn,' said Masha.

'Congratulations,' said Mr F.

'Ha,' said Josh, and grinned at the corner of the ceiling.

From that day, Josh was in the A-team. He was good at chess, and he was even better at finding out new ways of distracting his opponents. One week he would sniff really loudly, at precisely three-minute intervals. The next week he would push thumbtacks into the soles of his sneakers, and make a tapping sound every time his opponent was about to move. And today, there was a clicking noise coming from his direction – except nobody could work out how he was making it.

Mr F walked around the room, turning his head towards the clicking whenever it happened.

'Josh,' Mr F said eventually, loudly enough to make half the kids jump. 'Spit it out.'

Josh pretended he had no idea what Mr F was talking about.

'Josh.' It was a warning, and everyone knew what happened if you kept going after one of Mr F's warnings.

Josh leaned forward and spat out something that looked like a pair of short tweezers into his palm. He showed it to Mr F, then put it into his pocket.

'You are so gross,' Anna whispered. Josh grinned, letting the saliva dribble ever so slightly from the corner of his mouth.

'It's time to think and observe,' Mr F said. 'And what does that mean?'

'Silence,' they all said.

'That's right. And if I hear one more sound, you're all out. Do you understand?'

Everyone nodded. Even Josh.

'Now play.'

Anna was proud to be number one in the A-team of the chess squad.

By the end of last year, she'd been easily beating their previous number one, Patrick, in their matches. Now Patrick was at high school. Anna had asked Mr F if she could take over as number one, but Mr F had said, 'You beat Patrick because you knew his game.'

'So?' Anna had said. 'I still won.'

'It's not just about beating Patrick. You've got to beat the number ones from the other teams.'

'I'm better than most of them, Mr F. I've watched them, and I know I can beat them.'

'Technically, yes, you are better.' Mr F had

nodded. 'But you've got to pay more attention to what the other player is doing, not just think about your own game. Who said, "One day you give your opponent a lesson, the next day he gives you one"?'

'Don't know, sir.'

'Grandmaster Bobby Fisher,' Mr F had said. 'It's not about how good you are, it's about how well you can read your opponent.'

So Anna tried to take Mr F's advice and read her opponent, but in the end it didn't matter. Nobody could come close to beating her.

Right at the beginning of the school year, when Mr F had announced the team, Anna had rushed home to tell her parents.

'Mum, Dad,' she said, throwing her bag down in the hallway, 'I'm number one in the A-team!'

Anna went into the kitchen. Her mother was sitting at the kitchen table, working on her laptop; her father was chopping vegetables for dinner.

'Well done, sweetheart!' Anna's dad said, putting out his arms to her. 'I'm so proud of you!'

'Thanks, Dad,' Anna said.

Anna waited for her mother to say something. Her mother was hunched forward, the way she always was when she was concentrating. Anna's mother was a researcher at the university, and had won a big international prize for curing some tree fungus that had been causing lots of problems. When she was concentrating, it was like she was in another world. She probably hadn't even noticed that Anna had come home.

'Del?' Anna's father said. 'Anna's got some news.'

Anna's mother blinked, and looked up.

'Mum,' Anna said, 'I'm number one in the A-team. For chess.'

Anna's mum blinked again. Then she said, 'So you should be.'

Anna felt her father squeezing her shoulder.

'We're very proud of you,' Anna's father said. 'Aren't we, Del?'

Anna's mum looked at Anna's father.

'Yes, Anna,' she said. 'We're very proud of you.'

'Game of chess after dinner?' Anna asked.

Her mum nodded and said, 'Okay.'

Anna's mum was the one person Anna could never beat in chess. She could somehow work out exactly what Anna was planning to do, and then block her from doing it. She could never really understand how Anna felt about things, but when it came to chess it was as if she could read Anna's mind.

After the game had finished, Anna headed for her room.

'You're a good girl, Anna,' her father said.

'Thanks, Dad,' Anna replied. 'Chess makes everything better.'

'Josh,' Mr F said, 'if you make one more noise, you're out.'

Josh didn't look up, or even show that he was listening, but the high-pitched sound coming from his direction stopped.

'Good,' Mr F said. 'Next week is the first qualifier for you, A-team. I want you to annotate all of your games, and I want you to analyse them, and I want you to tell me where the weakness in your game is.'

'Even if we win?' asked Anna.

'Especially if you win,' Mr F said. 'If you win because of something your opponent let you get away with, I want you to tell me what you would have done if your opponent had done something different. And B- and C-teams, it won't hurt you to do the same.'

'Yes, sir,' the players said.

'A-team, you need to be especially vigilant. Because you're the reigning champions, your opposition will be working even harder to demolish you. Everybody wants that Chess Championship trophy, and nobody is entitled to it. Not even you.'

'But, sir?'

'Yes, Anna?' Mr F sighed. Anna always had a question.

'Masha is number two, and Josh is our number three.'

'That's correct.'

'Who's going to be our number four?'

'I don't know who the number four is, yet,' Mr F said. 'It'll have to be one of the reserves. We might have to rotate during the qualifiers.'

Anna said, 'But, sir, that's not fair. How can we have a decent team that way? Why can't we have Elias?'

Elias sat up straighter, returning to a slumped

position when Mr F said, 'Because Elias is number one for the B-team.'

'But we're more important,' Anna said.

'Are not,' grumbled Elias.

'Yeah,' said some of the kids from the B- and C-teams. 'I mean, nah.'

'All the teams matter equally,' Mr F said. 'Now, Anna, you play Masha. Josh, you can play Olivia today.'

Olivia was one of the reserves. She beamed and came and sat across from Josh, her notepad out, ready to write down who made what move when.

The room became quiet while everyone concentrated. Mr F walked around, watching silently, occasionally whispering advice to the B- or C-team players.

They were all so engrossed in their games that it was only towards the end of squad that they noticed Jackson at the edge of the chess room. Nobody knew how long he'd been there. He was peering over at the game between Anna and Masha.

'Jackson,' Mr F said in a normal voice, making

the chess players jump in their seats, 'you're quite welcome to come and sit down. You'll be able to see better then.'

The players all turned to stare at Jackson. Sporty kids like Jackson never came to chess. In the playground, Flash Buckley called the chess kids Chess Nuts.

'Hey, Chess Nuts,' he'd call. 'Want to play a real game?' Then he'd kick a soccer ball at their heads, or throw a cricket ball so it ricocheted just near their feet.

Sporty kids and chess kids did not mix.

So the squad stared at Jackson, and Jackson looked at the ground, mumbled, 'No thanks, sir,' and loped towards the door. His ears were hot. Hopefully nobody could see how red they were. Then he heard Anna say, 'What does he want? He probably doesn't even know how to play.'

'Yeah,' said some of the other kids.

Jackson wanted to come back in, sit down, and blitz them all, but how could he? Everyone knew Jackson was the best athlete in the school, and why would someone like that hang around the chess room? Jackson could imagine what Flash Buckley would think if he saw Jackson with the Chess Nuts.

I'll show them, Jackson decided.

Just not today.

Jackson bolted past the No Running sign. He was late for afternoon state swimming training; the pool was a blur of splashing arms and kicking feet, studded with various-coloured swimming caps representing swimmers from different schools.

'No running!' the coach yelled.

Jackson slowed down.

'Hurry up!' the coach yelled.

'Make up your mind,' Jackson muttered before tossing his bag down, kicking off his shoes, and peeling off his uniform.

He ambled to the end of the pool and stretched his arms over his head, first in one direction, then in the other.

'Second time in a row!' The coach kept up with his yelling, even though he was now right next to Jackson. 'Lost your watch, have you?'

Jackson shrugged and jumped in the pool. He moved near the lane ropes, out of the way of the swimmers doing their tumble turns, and made a big deal out of adjusting his goggles, until the coach moved over to one of the other lanes, yelling at one of the other swimmers about how slow she had taken the turn. Jackson was preparing to push off when someone kicked him in the stomach.

Flash Buckley.

Jackson doubled over with pain and fury. He wanted to swim after Flash and grab him, but he could barely breathe.

'Get moving, Jackson!' the coach bellowed.

'But sir, I – '

'Go!'

So Jackson pushed himself away from the wall, as hard as he could, considering his aching stomach, and started on his 500-metre freestyle. When he saw Flash Buckley coming towards him, on his second lap, Jackson veered into his lane. Jackson curled his hands into fists, ready to pummel Flash. The coach's whistle blew three times, the signal to freeze. Everyone stopped, no matter where they were in the pool, and waited for the coach's instructions. Flash was right next to Jackson, his eyes hidden behind his mirrored goggles.

'Jackson! What are you doing?'

'Yeah,' Flash repeated under his breath. 'What are you doing?'

Jackson kept his eyes on the coach and said, 'Nothing, sir.'

'Then stay in your own lane, and watch where you're going!'

Flash laughed loudly. The coach blew his whistle again, and everyone started swimming. Jackson swam fast, his arms slicing the water furiously.

'The state carnival's only a few weeks away,' the coach said to the team at the end of training. 'So you'll be training for an extra half an hour every morning and every afternoon.'

The squad groaned.

'I knew you'd be pleased to hear that.' The coach smiled. 'But I have a warning for all of you.'

He looked around at the team before his eyes rested on Jackson. 'If any of you are late more than three times, or miss three sessions of training, you're out. And no more horseplay in the pool, or there'll be trouble.'

Jackson turned his face away from the coach. Once upon a time, Jackson had arrived at all the training sessions a quarter of an hour early, eager to go. Now he felt the same way as he'd felt at the end of the cross-country. Empty. Like all of a sudden it didn't matter. Like he couldn't be bothered.

Jackson didn't go to the change rooms. He knew Flash Buckley would be there, waiting for a fight, and although Jackson usually ignored his taunts, today he wasn't sure he could control himself. Jackson knew Flash wanted to get him in trouble, and Jackson wasn't about to give him the pleasure. He pulled his clothes on over his wet bathers and walked home.

'Mum?' he yelled as he came in the front door.

There was no reply. He guessed his mum must have been called to work. He made himself a sandwich and ate it at the counter. Then he went down to his parents' room.

Jackson saw the flickering of the television, and he paused in the doorway.

'Dad?' he whispered.

His dad was lying on his back. This was the most comfortable position for him since the accident. Jackson couldn't see if his eyes were open or not, but then his dad said, 'Hi, son. How's it going?'

His voice was slurred and slow.

'Good, Dad.'

'Good.'

Jackson waited for his dad to ask him something, like he used to in the old days, when he knew what training he'd been to on what night, and which finals and championships were coming up, and who had won the latest qualifier, Jackson or Flash Buckley. But he didn't say anything.

'How about a game of chess, Dad?'

Jackson knew the answer, but he hoped that maybe, today, his dad would change his mind.

'Thanks, son, but I'm a bit tired today. Maybe another time.'

His dad hadn't played chess since the accident. Jackson's mum told him not to bother his father about things like that, so he didn't, mostly.

'It's okay, Dad,' Jackson lied.

Jackson missed playing proper chess. He played on his DS, and read books about tactics and strategy, but it wasn't the same as playing with someone. You needed to play someone better than you, who made you work hard to get them in tricky positions, who made you find a way to defend against an unexpected attack, someone who could explain what you did right and wrong after the game. Jackson had been getting good at chess, thanks to his dad's coaching, when the accident happened.

He thought about the game he'd watched today. Anna was good, but he'd seen a weakness that Masha had missed. Anna had left her queen open to attack. Jackson could tell she hadn't meant to do that, because she made her next move in a big hurry, clearly relieved that Masha was so worried about her own next move that she hadn't looked at the board carefully enough. But if Jackson had been playing, he would have seen it. He hated the way Anna looked at him with a superior expression, like because he played sports he must be dumb.

Jackson shook his head. He was supposed to be thinking about the swimming championships, not chess squad, where he wasn't even on a team.

His father started to snore. Jackson quietly closed the door, then went to his own room. He set up his chess set, and ran through the moves he remembered from Masha's game with Anna. Except, when he got to the point where Masha messed up, he took the queen. In four more moves, it would have been checkmate.

'Gotcha,' he said, and grinned.

It was the last week of chess practice before the qualifiers. Even though anyone was normally allowed to play chess from Monday to Wednesday, today Mr F said to the kids who were hoping for a game, 'You're welcome to come in and watch this week, but I'll only be coaching the squads.'

Some of the kids groaned and turned away; others went in anyway, and dragged a chair over to the tables. Anna, Josh and Masha were already at their boards, waiting to be told who would play who. And, most importantly, who was going to be their number four. If the three of them won their games in the qualifiers, it didn't matter. But if they tied, or lost, the fourth player was crucial.

But Mr F had them captive. It was time for one of his grandmaster stories. Anna rolled her eyes at Masha, but Masha only shrugged.

Anna wondered if Masha didn't understand how boring the stories were because her English wasn't that good. When she had arrived at school the year before, she hadn't been able to spell her name out loud when the teacher had asked her. All the class had laughed, except for Anna, who had said to Flash Buckley, sitting in front of her, 'Shut up, gizzard features.'

Masha had smiled at Anna, and from then on they had eaten their recess snacks together and gone to chess practice at lunchtime. Masha didn't say much apart from 'hmmmn' or 'yes' sometimes, and 'no, sir' when Mr F asked a question, and 'oh' when something surprised her, but Anna didn't mind that Masha was so quiet. Anna was delighted that Masha was already a strong chess player, although she was also relieved that Masha wasn't better than her.

'We're playing Condor South first up,' Mr F said. 'What do you remember about them from last year?'

'We aced them,' Anna said.

'Hah,' said Josh.

'Hmmn,' said Masha.

Mr F tsked. 'Who said, "It's just you and your opponent at the board and you're trying to prove something"?'

'Don't know, sir,' Anna said, even though she did.

'Grandmaster Bobby Fischer,' Mr F said. 'And if you think you don't have anything to prove to Condor South, you're in trouble.'

'Yes, sir.' Anna sighed. 'But, sir, what about the actual A-team? We still don't have a number four.'

'Don't rest on your laurels,' Mr F went on, ignoring Anna. ' "If you see a good move, look for a better one." Who said that?'

Before anyone had a chance to say, 'Don't know, sir,' a voice came from the back of the chess room.

'Grandmaster Emanuel Lasker.'

Everyone turned to see who it was.

And stared.

It was Jackson.

'That's right,' Mr F said. 'Welcome to squad, Jackson.'

'I'll go number four,' Jackson said. 'If you want.'

'Don't be stupid,' Anna sneered. 'We need a number four for the A-team, not for the beginner la-la team.'

'Anna,' Mr F said sternly. 'This is my squad, and I'll make the decisions, not you. Do you understand?'

'Yes, sir,' Anna replied. But she crossed her arms and slumped down in her chair.

She didn't know what a sporty kid like Jackson was doing in the chess room, even if he did know who said the thing about good moves. But if Mr F decided he was going to play, it meant one thing: the A-team would lose.

'Jackson,' Mr F said after a long pause, 'welcome to the A-team.'

Anna turned a strange shade of purple. Her hand shot in the air, and she barely waited for Mr F to say, 'What is it, Anna?' before she burst out with, 'But, sir, you can't.'

'I can. And I have.'

'What about Olivia?'

'Olivia is playing with the B-team.'

'What about – what about – '

'Anna,' Mr F said, 'stop arguing. My decision is final.'

'But, *sir*.'

Mr F sighed. 'What is it now, Anna?'

'You don't even know if he can play.'

Mr F looked at Jackson.

'Jackson,' Mr F said. 'Sit down here.'

He pointed to the chair opposite Anna's. Anna and Jackson both said, 'But, sir – '

Mr F put his hand up to silence them. ' "The only thing chess players have in common is chess," ' he said. 'Who said that?'

'Don't know, sir,' Anna snarled. 'I suppose *he* does.'

'No,' Jackson said. 'Not this time.'

'Grandmaster Lodewijk Prins.' Mr F smiled into the air, as if he'd forgotten why he was there, and then said, 'Play. Josh and Masha, watch.'

Anna was white; Jackson was black. Anna slumped in her chair, the way she did when she played kids from the junior school. She made a big deal of sighing, and took long drinks from her water bottle when it was her turn. She moved slowly, the way they were supposed to, but she looked as if she wasn't bothering to think.

Anna played the same opening as she had on the game with Masha, building the King's Indian Attack.

Jackson moved carefully, examining Anna's face after each turn to see if she saw what he was doing. They were near the middle of the game before Anna realised, and when she did, her face turned white. She sat up straight and stopped drinking water.

Jackson wondered if she would change her tactics, or whether she had analysed her game enough to realise where she'd gone wrong with Masha. Perhaps she'd thought that she won because she played a better game, not because Masha had made a fatal error, and she hadn't seen the vulnerable queen.

There was only one way to find out.

Anna played exactly the same moves as she had with Masha. Jackson knew that meant that she either remembered the game, or else these were her standard moves with the King's Indian Attack opening. Whatever it was, Jackson made sure he took stock of the board after each move, just in case there was something he hadn't counted on.

And then they came to the point in the game

where Anna had left her queen open, and Masha had missed it.

Anna peeled off her jumper, and Jackson could see the sweat at her hairline. She took so long to move that Josh started making a drumming noise under the chair.

'Silence,' Mr F said.

Jackson watched as Anna slowly picked up her queen and moved her to safety.

Masha breathed, 'Ohhh.'

Jackson sank into his chair.

Great, he thought. I analysed the game all right, but I didn't work out what to do if she didn't make that move.

Jackson decided to go on the attack. Moving the queen to safety had cost Anna some of her momentum, and that gave Jackson a slight advantage.

The other teams had finished their games, and came to watch Anna and Jackson battle it out. As they moved into the endgame, the players were equal in material; Anna had started out in the better position, but now she was on the defensive

46

and Jackson was trying to demolish her remaining structure so he could start closing in on the king.

Jackson and Anna both knew what was going to happen, but they kept playing to the end.

At checkmate, Jackson held out his hand to Anna. Anna looked as if she wasn't going to take it, but finally she gave it a curt shake, then wiped her palm on her skirt.

'Good game,' he said.

'You almost beat me,' she said.

'But I didn't.'

'No. You didn't.'

'It was fun.'

'It was okay.'

Jackson frowned at her. 'Listen,' he said hotly, 'you don't have to be so rude.'

'You played well, Jackson. Congratulations,' Anna said in a sarcastic voice. 'Is that what you want me to say?'

They stared at each other. Masha and Josh leaned forward. Chess players got tense with each other sometimes, but Anna was looking as if she wished Jackson would go away and never come back.

'Anna,' Mr F warned. 'Where is your chess etiquette?'

Anna put out her hand once more to Jackson and said, 'Good game,' although she still didn't sound sincere. Jackson warily shook her hand; Anna stood up and headed for the door.

'So,' Mr F said to Anna, 'do you concur with my wisdom?'

'Huh?'

'I mean, are you happy to have Jackson as number four in the A-team?' He looked at Josh and Masha. 'All of you?'

Josh grunted and pressed his hands together and Masha nodded at the floor. Anna called over her shoulder, 'We're desperate, aren't we?'

'That's as welcome as you get around here,' Mr F said to Jackson. 'Don't worry. She'll get over it.'

'That's fine,' Jackson said, but he didn't smile. He was pleased to be on the chess team, but who did Anna think she was? But then he thought, If I can cope with Flash Buckley, I can cope with Anna.

As if Mr F had read his mind, he said to Jackson, 'If you can cope with Anna, you'll probably cope with Condor South. Probably.'

'Thanks,' Jackson said. 'I think.'

'Why aren't you playing footy?' one of Jackson's mates, Andrew, asked.

'Um, I've got a sore throat,' Jackson said.

'Still?'

'Yeah,' Jackson nodded. 'It's bad.'

'Shame,' Andrew said. 'Flash is hard work.'

'Oh, well. See ya.'

'See ya.'

Jackson waited till Andrew had jogged away in the direction of the oval, then snuck around the back way to the chess room.

'Slower,' Mr F was saying as Jackson walked in. 'You can't play if you don't have time to think. If I notice you're playing speed chess against

Condor South in the first qualifier, you'll be out.'

'Sorry I'm late,' Jackson said.

'Just show me I shouldn't be sorry to have put you on the A-team and we'll call it quits.'

Mr F was joking, but Jackson was worried. It turned out that he wasn't as great at chess as he wanted to be. Sure, he'd almost won that first time against Anna, but that was because he'd seen her play that game before – and look what had happened when she'd done something he wasn't expecting. His games with Masha and Josh were uneven – sometimes he won, sometimes he lost. And every time he played Anna during practice, he lost. He could feel himself getting better, game by game, and he never made the same mistake twice, but Anna knew exactly what she wanted to do in a game and demolished his strategy as if his own game was totally obvious. He wondered if there was something he was doing that was too easy to read, the way Jackson could tell where a soccer player was aiming because of where he looked before the kick. He wished he had someone to ask, like his dad.

Anna leaned forward during all her games, the heels of her hands pressed into her forehead. She pressed so hard that by the end of each session she had two red marks that lasted for hours. Flash Buckley teased her and said they were where her devil-horns had fallen off, and she said, 'Don't be a vexatious ignoramus,' which wasn't as nasty as she wanted it to be, but she was too tired to come up with anything worse.

On the day before the first qualifier, Jackson was so busy checking out whether anyone was in sight of the chess room that he didn't notice Anna standing in the doorway, her arms crossed, blocking his entry.

'What are you doing?' she said.

'Nothing,' said Jackson.

'You don't want anyone to see you hanging round with us, do you?' Anna smiled. 'What a chicken.'

'You mean, like you don't want anyone to see you try at sport?' he said. 'What a chicken.'

Anna stared coldly at him, then turned on her heel and spat over her shoulder, 'Why don't you go back to what you're good at and leave me alone?'

Jackson beat Anna in chess for the first time that day. He should have felt happy about it, but he didn't. He only won because Anna was too offended by what he'd said to play properly, though nobody else would have noticed anything was wrong.

'Good game, Jackson,' Mr F said. 'Anna, you need to work on your defence. You're a brilliant attacker, but you need to be prepared in case things change when you're not expecting them. Kasparov said – '

'I don't care what Kasparov said,' Anna said. Then she looked at Jackson. 'He won't beat me again.'

'It was a lucky win, Mr F,' Jackson said.

Mr F shook his head. 'No such thing,' he replied. To the whole class he said, 'Now all of you, get some rest tonight. You don't know who's playing for Condor South, and I want you to be prepared for anything. Do you understand?'

'Yes, sir,' the players said.

Jackson tried to get Anna's attention before she went back to class, but she stormed away.

He shrugged and stepped out of the chess room, so preoccupied that he didn't notice Flash Buckley, or the smile that crawled across Flash's face when he saw Jackson.

'Anna,' her mother said as they were practising chess that evening, 'you are not thinking.'

'I am,' Anna protested, but then her mother pointed at the board and showed her the blunder she had just made. It was obvious – so obvious a grade four would have noticed.

'Oh,' Anna said. 'Can I take it back?'

'You can't take a move back,' her mother said. 'You know that.'

'Are you going to keep playing?'

'Five moves to checkmate. Game over.'

Anna sat and stared at the board, working out what the five moves would be.

'Hey, sweetheart,' her dad said eventually.

'Better get to bed – need to be rested for your first qualifier, eh?'

Anna hadn't noticed that her mother had gone. She was sitting at the chessboard alone, and it was past nine o'clock.

'We'll win anyway,' Anna said. 'At least, we will if our new number four doesn't mess it up for us.'

Anna's father peered at her. 'Are you all right?'

Anna thought about Jackson calling her a chicken. It made her angry, but it also made her feel prickly with shame, because it was true. She was scared of trying at sport because Flash Buckley had teased her, simple as that.

'Sort of,' Anna said.

'Anything I can help with?'

'I'm too tired to explain.'

'Then go to bed,' her father said, prodding her shoulder. 'Chess can wait until tomorrow.'

'It's not chess I'm worried about.'

Her father frowned. 'Then what is it?'

'I was mean to someone today,' Anna said. 'And then they were mean back.'

'Well, maybe you could apologise tomorrow.'

'Maybe,' Anna said, then yawned. 'Good night, Dad.'

But she couldn't sleep. She thought about apologising to Jackson, but she knew she couldn't. It was too late, like wanting to take a move back in chess.

Because Phoenix had won their A-team finals the year before, Condor South travelled to Phoenix for Qualifier One. As the Phoenix players waited for Condor South to arrive, Mr F spoke to them.

'You need to take your time, players,' he said. 'Watch your opponents. Make sure each move you make has a strategy behind it.'

The chess players listened and nodded, but secretly Anna wasn't too worried. Last year, Condor South's A-team was made up of four boys who had assumed they would win, and Phoenix had finished them off in record time.

'"One bad move ruins forty good ones,"' Mr F continued. 'Who said that?'

'International Master Al Horowitz, sir,' Jackson said. He glanced over at Anna to see if she might be a bit impressed, but Anna, not realising he was looking, pulled a face to herself.

'Correct,' Mr F said. 'So you need to pay attention to each move, even if you think you know exactly what the best move is.' Mr F nodded at the door, and said, 'Good luck, teams, and don't forget to annotate your games.'

Anna's first shock was that Condor South's A-team was not the same as last year's. Sure, she expected that a couple of the boys had moved on to high school, but not that there would be an entirely new team. This year, there were four new players, all girls. Anna recognised one of the girls, Sophie, from a chess master class she'd gone to last year, and swallowed hard. If she was the number one, Anna was in trouble.

Sophie sat down opposite Anna.

'You're number one?' Anna asked.

'Duh,' Sophie said, arranging her chess notation pad neatly by the board. When she looked up at Anna, she said, 'Good luck,' in a way that didn't sound like she was wishing Anna luck at all.

Anna had started off the day feeling tired and tense, and now she felt sick as well.

Sophie drew white, and set up the Queen's Gambit, which Anna could accept by taking the pawn on C4.

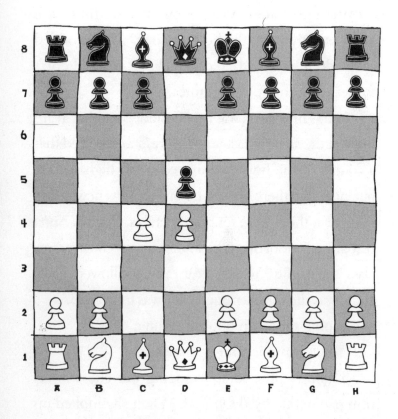

But Anna didn't take the pawn. Instead, she moved her pawn on E7 to E6. When Sophie moved her knight to C3, Anna was confident she had succeeded in setting up the Elephant Trap, which tricked white into losing one of its pieces. She mentally played the game ahead. If Sophie fell for the trap, Anna would be able to back her into a corner in no time. Anna moved her knight to F6 and waited.

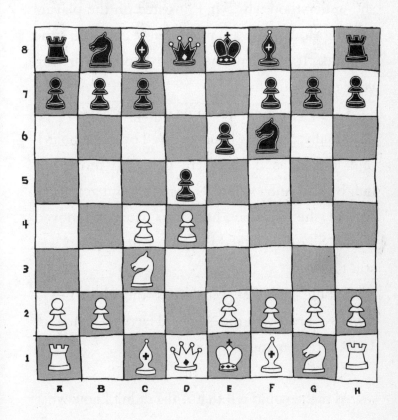

It was Sophie's turn to play the crucial move that would lead her into the trap. Anna watched her eyes, to see if she was working out what would happen if she took the bait of the pawn on D5. Sophie's gaze ranged around the board, and Anna's palms were sweaty with anticipation: would she, or wouldn't she? For the first time she understood why Mr F insisted on the players moving slowly. It wasn't just that it gave you time to think. It also had the added bonus of driving your opponents mad.

Come on, come on, Anna thought. Move!

Finally, Sophie's hand hovered over the board. She looked as if she were going to move her knight, and Anna stopped breathing. But at the last second, she picked up her king's pawn and moved it out. She didn't take the bait; Anna's pawn was still there.

Sophie smiled at Anna across the table. 'Good try. I've practised the Mayet–Harrwitz game of 1848, too, you know.'

'Oh. Sure.'

As if she could tell that Anna didn't know what

she was talking about, Sophie said, 'Where the Elephant Trap comes from.'

Anna was thinking that the only place she'd seen the Elephant Trap was on YouTube when Mr F came up and hissed, 'Silence!'

Anna looked at the board in panic. She'd been so confident that Sophie would take the bait, and then so impatient when she was taking so long to move, that she didn't have a second strategy. With Sophie's pieces already out on the board, and with the moves she'd wasted setting up the trap, Anna searched and searched for a way to create some momentum. She couldn't move her bishop out to check the king; the only move she could make was to defend herself from attack.

The game was already over, but they had to play it out to checkmate anyway.

'Well done,' Anna said reluctantly.

'Next time,' Sophie said, 'you could try giving me a challenge.'

Anna really wanted to get rid of Sophie's smug, know-it-all smile. She got up from the board and wandered around to see how the rest of the A-team was doing, because she was afraid that if she spent one more minute looking at Sophie she'd throw water in her face.

Josh had lost.

Masha had lost.

And Jackson was about to lose, too. He sat at the board, frowning, and his opponent was taking her time over her move, even though Jackson had no chance. His king was backed into a corner, and he had lost his queen. All the girl needed to do was bring down her rook and move her queen one square closer, and it was checkmate. Jackson was looking desperately at the board in case he had missed something, but once she edged her queen closer Jackson laid down his king and held out his hand.

'Good game,' he said.

'Yes,' she replied, and then skipped off to her captain.

Mr F took a deep breath, shook the other chess coach's hand, and said, 'Thanks for coming. Hope to see you in the finals.'

The Condor South players sauntered to their

bus, laughing and chattering excitedly, ignoring the Phoenix players. Anna sat at Jackson's table.

'The B- and C-teams won,' Anna said.

'Yeah?' Jackson said.

'We've been humiliated,' she said.

Jackson didn't reply, but just sat there fiddling with the king. Masha and Josh pulled up extra chairs and waited for Mr F in silence. Even Josh, for once, was quiet.

Mr F congratulated the B- and C-teams and sent them to their classrooms. Then he turned to the A-team and said, 'I don't know what you were doing – I've never seen such a dreadful display. Anna, you were playing too fast. Josh, you were so busy trying to distract your opponent that you distracted yourself. Masha and Jackson, you came closest, but you both made obvious errors in your end games. What's the matter with you all?'

'Don't know, sir,' Anna muttered.

'Sorry, sir,' Jackson mumbled.

'You don't listen to the grandmasters, that's fine,' he said. 'You don't listen to what I'm telling you in squad, that's fine.' He looked thoughtful for a moment and said, 'Actually, that's not fine, but we'll forget about that for now. But you all committed the cardinal sin of chess – you came to the board thinking you were going to win. Am I right?'

'Yes, sir,' Anna said miserably.

'Yes, sir,' Josh said, rocking in his chair.

'Maybe, sir,' Jackson said.

'Hmmn,' Masha said.

'There's only one thing for it,' Mr F said. 'A-team will practise every day after school,' – he held up his hand at their groan – 'until the finals. Starting today. If we don't win this last qualifier, we're out of the semifinals. This school has never missed out on the semis, and we're not going to start now – not if I've got anything to do with it.'

'But, sir,' Jackson said, 'I have swimming squad.'

'Well, Jackson,' Mr F said. 'You'll have to make a decision, won't you?'

'But – '

'No buts. I'll see you all here at 3.00 p.m. Sharp.'

Jackson turned up early to morning swimming training. There were only a few kids there, standing at the end of the pool, warming up while they waited. One of them looked at Jackson, pulled a face, and drew his finger across his throat. That meant Jackson was in serious trouble.

Jackson had thought about turning up after chess practice, the day before, but he figured he'd be better off missing it altogether. When he saw the coach, his stomach tingled with nerves.

'Jackson, pleased you've decided to grace us with your presence,' the coach said, filling out something on a clipboard. 'You have a sick note for yesterday?'

'No, sir.'

The coach raised his eyebrows, but didn't look up from his paperwork.

'I wanted to ask something,' Jackson said.

'Out with it.'

'Could I – if I – what if – '

The coach sighed. He tucked the clipboard under his arm and looked straight at Jackson.

'I haven't got all day.'

'Well,' said Jackson, 'the thing is, I can't get to afternoon practice. So, well, what if I come extra early in the mornings, and make up the time?'

The coach just stood there, staring at Jackson the way he looked at kids who couldn't swim fast enough, or who got puffed halfway through training sessions, or who accidentally fell off the starting blocks before a race started. The coach had never looked at Jackson like that before, and Jackson didn't like it. He could feel the other kids standing nearer, trying to listen in.

Then the coach laughed a dry, humourless laugh. 'You are joking,' he said. The laugh stopped as suddenly as it started. 'Aren't you?'

'Um, no,' Jackson said. 'I just thought, well, it'd be the same time – '

'Are you in this squad or aren't you?' the coach said.

'In?' Jackson said.

'So you come to afternoon practice, on time, like everyone else,' the coach said. 'End of story.'

The coach turned and walked off. Jackson called after him, 'But, sir. I can't.'

Jackson wasn't sure if the coach heard him, at first. But then he slowly turned back.

'I can't,' Jackson said, again.

The coach's chest rose, as if he were about to yell, but instead he said, in a slow, low, menacing voice, *'Why – not?'*

Jackson tried to think of an excuse. He couldn't tell the coach in front of everyone. People like Jackson didn't play chess. Everyone knew that only smart kids, or misfits, or kids who didn't know what else to do at lunchtime played chess. If he told the swim squad, what would they think?

'He can't swim,' came a voice, 'because he's playing chess.'

The swim squad all began to talk excitedly. Jackson turned around, even though he knew who'd spoken.

Flash Buckley.

Flash was grinning at Jackson. His eyes had turned into glinting slits as he looked around. He was enjoying the commotion. Jackson thought about going over and giving him a good whack, but he knew if he did he'd be in even more trouble.

'Be quiet!' the coach bellowed.

The chatter stopped, but Jackson could feel the other swimmers looking at him.

'Is this true?' the coach said. 'You've joined a – *chess* team?'

'Yes, sir,' Jackson said.

'A school chess team?'

'Yes.'

'A school chess team that's practising at the same time as the state swim squad?'

'Yes, sir,' Jackson said, then added, 'It's the A-team.'

'I don't care whether it's the Kasparov genius dream team!' the coach said. 'You're out.'

'What?'

'Go,' the coach said. 'This is an elite squad, as you know perfectly well. I don't want people here unless they're serious. You're not. Go.'

Jackson paused. He had thought the coach might be angry with him for missing some training, but he didn't imagine that he'd be kicked out altogether. Last year, Jackson had won the national trophy for the hundred-metres freestyle, and he had been part of the winning relay team. The only person who could beat Jackson, if Jackson was having a bad day, was Flash Buckley. The coach couldn't kick him out. Could he?

'Out of here,' the coach said. Then he turned to the swimmers, who were motionless with shock, and said, 'Two hundred freestyle, followed by two hundred backstroke, then we'll do some relay practice. Go!'

Jackson moved slowly away. He felt numbed, as if he'd jumped into freezing water. He was almost at the turnstiles when he turned and took one last look.

Flash Buckley hadn't jumped in the pool with

everyone else. He was staring at Jackson. If Jackson wasn't in condition, that would mean Flash would win the championships, and would be Outstanding Athlete of the Year. It was what Flash had always wanted.

But Flash didn't look pleased. He looked as shocked as Jackson.

'You've come back,' Mr F said to Jackson, as he walked into after-school squad.

Jackson shrugged, and sat down at the first table.

'I got a call from your swimming coach this morning,' Mr F said, then he shook his head. 'Got quite a command of the vernacular, hasn't he?'

'What?' Jackson said.

'He was spectacularly rude.' Mr F smiled. 'Said I was ruining his championships, and depriving you of your chance to be Outstanding Athlete. I pointed out that you'd been Outstanding Athlete before, but you've never been a member of a winning chess team. Strangely, he didn't appreciate my argument.'

Jackson kept his eyes on the board. Mr F examined him for a moment, and then turned to Anna, Masha and Josh.

'Right, A-team,' he said. 'You have two weeks to improve your form. I want you eating, drinking, thinking, living chess. If you lose the next qualifier, that's it.'

The A-team was quiet for the rest of the session. Josh didn't make any strange noises, Masha didn't sigh, and Anna didn't argue. If Mr F asked, 'Who said . . .', Jackson didn't offer an answer. And when Mr F told them who had said it, they listened.

They analysed their Condor South games one by one, and if they couldn't work out where they had blundered, Mr F showed them. Anna growled to herself with frustration when she realised how she could have avoided Sophie's attack; she'd let Sophie get to her. She should have seen it three moves before it started.

Mr F paired Anna and Jackson and told them to practise the English opening. Anna said, 'Hi', Jackson said, 'Hi', and then they played without even looking at each other. Jackson was frowning, and when Anna beat him, he frowned even more. Anna tried talking to him afterwards.

'Good game,' she said.

'For you,' Jackson said.

'You just missed the bishop attacking your rook,' Anna said.

Jackson didn't reply, so Anna went on. 'That's why even though bishops have the same weighting as knights, I reckon bishops are better, because – '

'I hate missing things,' Jackson said.

'It's just practice,' Anna said. 'Like how you train before you win a race.'

'What would you know?' Jackson stood up so suddenly his chair fell over. 'Just – just leave me alone.'

'Jackson,' Mr F said sternly. 'Don't you speak like that to your team-mate.'

Jackson strode off outside and grabbed his bag off the hook. He started to rush off again, and then he stopped.

Anna went up to the doorway, thinking she would shout something after him, but then she saw him take his bag off his shoulder. Something was painted on the outside of Jackson's bag, but it was in smeary letters, and Anna couldn't read what it said. He lifted the gear out of his bag, one by one – books, lunchbox, pencil case. They were covered in something sticky and pink. Then he lifted out a six-pack of yoghurt with all the tops ripped open.

At first, Anna wondered why Jackson would bring so many yoghurts to school, before she realised that he wouldn't.

Somebody had put the yoghurts there. Somebody really mean.

But who would do that to Jackson?

Jackson wiped his school things on the grass and put them back in his bag. He left the yoghurt containers on the grass, and marched away. As he went, Anna finally made out the words on his bag: *Chess Nut*.

Jackson was quiet for the next week, in chess practice and in class as well. Anna didn't try talking to him again. Every day she was surprised when he came to practice. And relieved. If they had any chance of winning, it had to be with Jackson. He was better than Josh and Masha most of the time, and it was only because he made blunders in the endgame that Anna beat him.

Two days before the second qualifier, the class was working on a Society and Environment project about Australian explorers. Halfway through a discussion about Burke and Wills, the teacher darted out to get something she'd forgotten. The minute she left, everyone started talking and laughing. And in the middle of the commotion, Flash Buckley stood up at the front of the class.

'Hey Jackson,' he said. 'We miss you at training. We really do.'

Everyone craned around to look at Jackson, who was slumped at his desk at the back of the class, writing something in his notebook. He ignored Flash, and pretended he didn't know that everyone was watching.

'I just don't get it,' Flash went on. 'Why do you want to hang around with the losers and retards playing chess?' Flash said 'chess' as if it was some kind of swear word.

'Shut up, Flash.' Jackson sounded bored, but Anna saw that his ears were pink.

'I knew you were lying about being sick,' Andrew said.

'Sorry,' said Jackson.

'Chess,' Flash's friend Ben said with a laugh. 'What would you do that for?'

Jackson stopped writing, and his hand made a fist around the pen. His lips were pressed firmly together.

'What about the swimming championships?' said Andrew.

'What about our house?' said Chelsea.

'What about the Outstanding Athlete of the Year?' said Ben.

The class started talking again – about Jackson. Flash stood at the front of the class, his arms crossed, grinning, waiting for Jackson to do something. Like he was inviting Jackson to fight him, right then, right there in the class.

'Leave him alone, you Neanderthal,' shouted Anna, suddenly and loudly. The class stopped looking at Jackson and turned her way.

Flash laughed. 'Oh, I get it.' He pursed his lips and made a loud kissing sound. 'Jackson's playing chess because Anna's his girlfriend.'

Everyone shrieked with laughter – at Jackson, at Anna, at the chess team.

'Just because you're too dumb to play, you gonad!' she snapped.

'Oooh,' Flash put his hand to his heart. 'I'm so hurt.' He looked at Jackson and said, 'Jackson, your girlfriend's being mean to me.'

Then someone hissed, 'Teacher's coming!'

Flash sat down in his place, and the class became perfectly quiet, pretending to work.

The teacher entered, looking around suspiciously. The only time her class was that quiet was if they'd been up to something. But nothing looked out of place, so she handed out photocopied maps of where Burke and Wills had trekked, and sat down, watchful. Anna wanted to turn and look at Jackson, except she didn't want the whole class to notice. Instead, she glanced over at Masha, who shook her head sympathetically.

'Poor Jackson,' Anna whispered.

'Yes,' Masha whispered back.

'What's that, Anna?' asked the teacher.

'Nothing, miss,' Anna said.

Jackson didn't turn up at chess practice after school that day; the next day he didn't even turn up to lunchtime practice. Anna tried to find a way to talk to him, to ask him if he was going to make the qualifiers or not, but every time he saw her coming he looked really busy, or suddenly got up and moved somewhere else.

'You and your boyfriend had a fight?' Flash said.

'Shut up, pond scum,' said Anna.

Later, as they were walking to chess practice, she said to Masha, 'What if he doesn't come to the qualifiers?'

'Hmmmn,' Masha said.

'We'll have to use a reserve. It'll be a disaster.'

'Hmmmn.'

'I *hate* Flash Buckley.'

'Yes,' said Masha loudly.

This was about the most Masha ever spoke, and other kids had given up trying to have conversations with her, but not Anna. She knew Masha understood things, and that was enough for her.

In the chess room, Mr F asked, 'Is Jackson sick?'

'Don't know, sir,' everyone said.

'Olivia, you'll be the number four in the A-team tomorrow,' Mr F said.

Olivia smiled happily. 'Thank you, sir.'

Mr F was silent for a while, then he said, '"Becoming successful at chess allows you to discover your own personality." Who said that?'

'Don't know, sir,' everyone said.

'International Chess Master Saudin Robovic,' Mr F said. 'I wonder if Jackson knows that.'

The chess players travelled to Barton school, and the A-team were as prepared as they could be. And they were determined, because losing meant missing out on the semifinals. Mr F was grim as they drove to Barton; the A-team was grimmer. The B- and C-teams were laughing and joking at the back of the bus, because even if they were decimated they were already through to the semis. Halfway to Barton, Anna turned around and snapped, 'Be quiet! Some of us need to concentrate!'

Callum, one of the C-team players replied, 'Just because you suck doesn't mean we all suck, Anna!'

Mr F braked so suddenly that Anna's seatbelt jerked tight over her ribs and shoulder.

'Chess squad,' he thundered, 'may I remind you that you are playing for your school, not just your team?'

'Yes, sir,' everyone muttered.

'Sorry, Anna,' Callum added.

'I want you all to prepare yourselves – and that means what, Olivia?'

'Quiet, sir.'

'That's right. Quiet.'

Barton school was much bigger than Phoenix, and their chess coach looked down his nose at the Phoenix players when they wandered in to the library. All of the Barton players were seated, motionless, at their tables, and they didn't smile or greet their opponents.

Anna's opponent was a boy who looked as if he were about eight. He didn't seem worried that Anna was so much older than him, but nor did he seem dismissive that she was a girl, the way most boys did. Anna craned around to see Masha, Josh and Olivia, who was their number four, and they were all playing boys who looked just as serious – and young – as Anna's opponent. Olivia looked terrified.

If only Jackson were here, Anna thought. He should be here. If they lost today, she would be the one dumping yoghurt in his bag.

Anna tried to act confident, but she drew black, and so she would not be going first. The boy moved his rook's pawn to A3, an unusual opening. She countered with C5, but she wasn't sure if it was the best response. What was he trying to do?

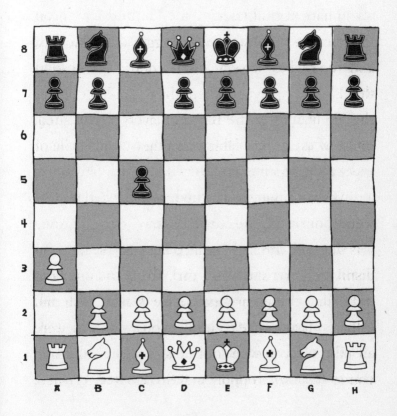

Anna watched the boy's eyes range over the board before each turn, but he rarely moved where she expected, and she was caught between trying to attack, her usual mode, and trying to defend. He didn't say one word, didn't make one sound, didn't even show he was aware that he was sitting across from another player. In the background she heard one of the other boys say, 'Excuse me, coach, my opponent is distracting me.' It must have been Josh he was playing, but Anna was trying so hard to concentrate that she didn't dare turn around to see.

The game seemed to go on forever; Anna was aware of the other players coming to stand around and watch, which meant they'd finished. She didn't look up once; her neck ached, and her behind was sore from sitting still for so long.

She and the boy went piece for piece, until finally they were left with two pawns and one king each. But although they were equal in material, Anna saw from the way the pawns were locked in, and the placement of her king, that he would be able to take her second-last pawn for free. When it was the boy's turn to move he looked up at her for the first time, waiting for her to lay down her king, admit defeat.

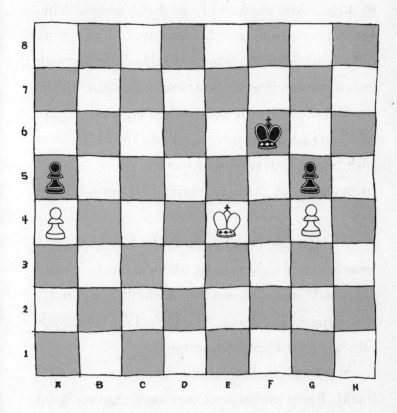

Anna paused. She looked at the board, willing it to show her a winning move, reveal something she had missed. She went through every combination of moves and results, but there was only one.

She felt sick. Phoenix had never missed out on the finals before. But if they missed out this year, it was her fault. She was number one – the leader of the A-team, the best player in the school. What had happened to her?

She laid down her king, and shook hands with her opponent. For the first time, he smiled.

'Good game,' she said grudgingly.

'You blundered at move fifteen,' he said.

'Aaron,' the coach said.

'Good game,' the boy said, then ran off to his team-mates.

Anna looked up. She saw Josh, who was moving from foot to foot, grinning, which meant he'd won. She saw Masha, who was looking modestly pleased, which meant she'd won. She looked for Olivia, but Olivia was nowhere to be seen.

'Mr F?' she said fearfully.

Mr F sent the other players away, then sat down next to Anna.

'The boy was right,' Mr F said. 'Move fifteen lost your momentum. Up until then you'd managed against the odds to have a positional advantage, but – '

'I mean, how did we go? The team?'

Mr F didn't smile. 'Well, Olivia tied – only because the other player was so busy gloating that he let her get in stalemate. So you're through to the semis.'

Anna was relieved, but only for a second.

'But Anna,' he said in a low voice, 'For the semis, I'm putting Masha at number one. Your concentration is all over the place – and you're so busy planning your own moves you miss what your opponent is doing. I'm sorry, but I have to think of the team.'

Anna felt as if something had stabbed her chest.

'No,' she said. 'You can't.' Her voice rose. 'I'm number one. I'm the best player. I can't – '

'We'll talk about this later,' Mr F said.

On the way back in the bus, all of the teams were chattering with delight. The C- and A-teams had won; the B-team had lost, but they were still set for the semifinal because of their unbroken wins during the qualifiers.

But Anna was miserable. She stared out the window all the way back. She couldn't even look at Masha, even though she'd said a sympathetic 'Hmmmn' to Anna.

It was so unfair. Anna had worked hard to be number one, and now it was being taken away from her, just like that. But she also knew that there was something wrong with her game, something she didn't know how to fix.

And without Jackson, there was a big chance that the A-team was going to tank in the finals.

Back home, the moment Anna walked in the door, her father said, 'Well, honey, how'd you go? Did you knock 'em dead?'

Her mother looked up from her computer, and her father explained, 'The last chess qualifier. It was today.'

'Oh,' Anna's mother said. 'Did you win?'

Anna dumped her bag on the floor, rustled around until she found the scrappy piece of paper with her notations on it, and pushed it across the table to her mother.

'The A-team won,' Anna said. 'Week after next are the semis.'

'Well,' her father said, 'that's good. Isn't it?'

Her mother's eyes scanned the moves, and then she shook her head.

'Move fifteen,' her mother said. 'You know better than this.'

'I just – ' Anna shrugged. 'I don't know.'

'You were not concentrating.'

'I was!'

'It's not possible. Look at where his knight was.'

'It was a mistake.'

'There are too many mistakes lately, Anna. You are too emotional.'

'At least I have feelings!' Anna shouted. 'Not like you!'

Anna stormed to her room and threw herself on her bed, weeping. What was she going to do?

Jackson was running. He was running around the school oval, long after school was out. He wasn't practising for anything, he wasn't competing for anything. He was just running.

Last night, he'd thought that maybe he could tell his dad about Flash, and about the chess team, and ask him what he should do. Even though his dad didn't feel like talking, maybe he wouldn't mind listening. But as soon as Jackson sat down in his dad's darkened room, he felt stupid. Why would his dad want to know? So when his dad said, 'All right, son?' Jackson said, 'Yeah, Dad.' He sat there for a while, but his father didn't ask anything more, and after a time Jackson left.

So now, Jackson ran, and tried to notice only the hiss of his breath in his ears, the springy crunch of the grass as he ran, the coolness as the breeze dried his sweat. He gazed at the scraggly bunch of trees at the edge of the oval, the clear spring sky above their waving leaves, and he breathed in the afternoon smell of warm grass. And then, without meaning to, he thought about chess.

He thought about the last game he'd played, the one he'd lost against Condor South. In chess squad, with Mr F's help, he'd worked out where he'd gone wrong, but he still hadn't worked out how he could have won. His opponent had been too aggressive, and none of Jackson's defences had been good enough.

Now it came to him, as obvious as if he was watching the replay of a grandmaster's game on the internet. There, then there, then there.

Checkmate!

Jackson stopped. He leaned his hands on his knees until his breath slowed down. He played through the moves again in his mind, to check. Yes. If only he'd moved his pawns up, and got his pieces out earlier, and sacrificed his queen! If only he could play the game again, he'd win this time.

But he wouldn't be playing any games again.

Jackson straightened up. He took a deep breath, and put his hands on his hips. And saw someone marching towards him from the trees.

Jackson's heart jolted, as if he'd started running again. If it was Flash, he was going to pummel him. He felt his fists curl at his sides, getting ready.

But when the figure came closer, Jackson saw that it wasn't Flash, or any of Flash's mates. It was a girl. Anna.

What did she want?

Anna had finally come to a decision. She didn't want to do it, but she had to. And she had to do it now.

'Hi,' Jackson said uncertainly. 'How'd you go yesterday?'

'I lost,' Anna said. 'And Olivia almost lost.'

'Oh,' Jackson said. 'So the A-team – '

'Yes. But only just.'

'Right,' Jackson said. 'I'm sorry I wasn't there.'

'Sorry?' Anna stood with her hands on her hips. 'You let us down.'

Jackson shrugged.

'Don't you care?'

'Well, yeah,' Jackson said. 'But you got some-one else.'

'That's not the point,' Anna said. 'It's a team. You wouldn't have let down your stupid soccer mates like that, would you?'

Jackson shrugged again.

Anna leaned forward. 'Are you scared of Flash Buckley?'

Jackson snorted. 'Of course not.'

'So why have you dropped out?'

'I don't know.' Jackson kicked a tuft of grass with his toe. 'Anyway, how come you lost your game? Were they that good?'

'I don't know either,' Anna said. 'I can't seem to concentrate anymore, or something. I try, but everything goes blurry.'

'Oh,' Jackson said.

'But I'm the captain of the team, no matter what,' Anna said. 'Even if Mr F does make Masha number one next week, I've been number one all year, and – '

'He's putting Masha at number one?' Jackson said. 'But you're way better than her.'

'Was,' Anna said. 'She won her last two qualifiers.'

'Still,' Jackson said.

'I'm only as good as my last games,' Anna said. 'And my last games were awful. That's why I'm here.'

Jackson laughed. 'I can't help you with your chess.'

'I wasn't asking that,' Anna said impatiently.

'So?'

Anna took a deep breath. 'The thing is, I'm the captain. And if we lose the finals, it's my responsibility. This year was my one and only go at number one, and if we blow it, that's it. And even if I can't play properly anymore, I want the A-team to have the best team. The best chance of winning. All of us.'

She spoke quickly, and Jackson understood how nervous she was, how hard it was for her to ask him. She was forcing herself to be humble, and humble didn't come naturally to Anna.

Jackson was silent for a while. Finally he said, 'I'm sorry, Anna. I just can't.'

Anna blinked at him for a moment, as if she couldn't believe what he was saying. Then her face turned pink.

'What do you mean, *you can't*?' she said, 'Why not?'

Jackson thought about telling her some of the reasons why, even if they weren't too clear in his own head, but the look on her face – as if she were stopping herself kicking his shins – stopped him.

'Fine,' she said. 'Fine! See if I care!' She stomped off, and then turned around and called, 'You're a bad sport, Jackson. I hate you – even more than I hate Flash Buckley!'

For the two weeks until the semifinals, Anna sulked. She sulked at school, she sulked at home. She sulked in spite of the spring sunshine that made everyone else happy. She sulked through lunchtime chess squad and after-school chess practice. But sulking didn't improve her game. Masha beat her more often than she ever had before, and when Mr F confirmed that Masha was number one for the semis, Anna didn't say anything, but only sulked a little more.

The school's swimming carnival was two days before the semifinals. Anna took a chessboard along, balanced it on the metal bench and practised with Masha while all the kids around her barracked for their houses. Even though she was resentful that Masha was number one, she wasn't so resentful that she didn't want to play chess. But every time she took one of Masha's major pieces, or won a game, she thought to herself, I wish Mr F was here to see that. I should *so* be number one. And then she thought, How come I can beat Masha in practice, but I can't win in the comps?

Anna hated swimming carnivals even more than cross-country, but at least this time nobody was forcing her to participate. Being crammed on the bus with noisy, excited kids, sitting in the uncomfortable, slatted benches in the stands, and being expected to squint at the aqua oblong with kids racing pointlessly up and down gave her a headache. She knew other people thought she was a bad sport for hating swimming carnivals so much, and that only made it worse.

Anna's one point of interest in the entire day, besides chess, was the final individual medley. This was the medley Flash Buckley was desperate to win, because if he won he would be Outstanding Athlete of the Year.

'I wonder if Jackson will swim,' Anna said to Masha.

'Hmmmn,' said Masha.

'I mean, he can still compete, even if he stopped going to state squad, can't he?'

Masha shrugged.

'If Flash wins Outstanding Athlete of the Year, he'll be even more hideous than he normally is.' Anna sighed.

'Hmmmn,' said Masha, with feeling.

Anna hadn't seen Jackson anywhere. He wasn't sitting with his house, and she didn't remember having seen him on any of the buses. She tried to identify who was on the starting blocks, but the glare from the water made it too hard. She could see swimming caps showing the colour of the houses, and that there was a boy and a girl for each house, and that was all.

Then a voice over the crackly PA announced who was in each lane. Flash Buckley was in lane five for Cook. Anna saw him snap his cap, like real swimmers did in the Olympics, and then shake out his arms and legs, hands and feet.

What a show-off, thought Anna.

But when the announcer finally called the competitors for Macquarie, there was no Jackson. Anna was disappointed. Who was going to put Flash Buckley in his place now?

The race began, and seemed to go on forever. It was so noisy with cheering and clapping that Anna couldn't concentrate on her chess. Eventually, she and Masha stood up in order to see what was happening.

Chelsea and Flash Buckley were way ahead of the other swimmers. As they came into the final freestyle laps, they were only a body length apart – and Chelsea was ahead.

'Yes!' Anna shrieked. 'Flash Buckley's going to be beaten – by a girl!'

Anna had never cheered before in her life. Chelsea wasn't even in her house, but she yelled her name until her throat hurt.

They came into the final lap. Every kid in the school was on their feet, chanting. Chelsea and Flash were exactly even, it seemed to Anna. She willed Chelsea to go faster.

'Please beat him,' Anna begged. 'Come on!'

But in the final twenty-five metres, Flash pulled ahead. Anna groaned. Flash touched the end of the pool two seconds before Chelsea.

'Noooo!' Anna wailed, holding her head in her hands. 'Flash Buckley – Outstanding Athlete of the Year! Ew!'

The swimmers climbed out of the pool. Anna saw Ms S shake Flash Buckley's hand, then Chelsea's. Chelsea waved at the crowd, and the crowd cheered back. Anna was waiting for Flash Buckley to flex his muscles, or hold his arms up to the crowd like some gladiator, the way he normally did if he won, but he just got his towel and went to the change rooms. Anna supposed there would be plenty of time for him to gloat, once they made the announcement.

When the screaming and cheering had calmed down, Ms S said over the PA, 'And now, the moment we've all been waiting for. Today, as you know, was the final component of the Outstanding Athlete of the Year award.'

The school clapped and whistled.

'Our athletes have worked hard for this award. Boys and girls have had to compete in a team game, the athletics, the cross-country and now the swimming. It's been a tough competition – and a close one.'

'Not as close as it should have been,' Anna muttered to Masha. 'Not if Jackson had been here.'

'But now, I am pleased to announce, the winner of this year's Outstanding Athlete of the Year . . .'

'Please let it be Chelsea,' Anna said. 'Maybe they did it on times, rather than winning?'

'Hmmmn,' said Masha, but she shook her head.

'The Outstanding Athlete of the Year is – Cook's champion, Flash Buckley!'

Cook jumped up and down, waving their flag and banners. The other houses cheered politely. When it had been Jackson, Anna remembered, the whole school had gone wild.

But Flash Buckley didn't appear. Ms S stood by the podium, waiting. She waited and waited. Everyone started chattering. Where was Flash Buckley?

'Okay, Phoenix,' Ms S said eventually. 'We'll go on to give the runner-up award for Outstanding Athlete of the Year – Chelsea!'

The school cheered more for Chelsea than they had for Flash. Ms S went on to give out all the other awards – the Best Sport Award, the Participation Award, and the All Rounder award – but still Flash Buckley didn't appear.

'I wonder what happened to Flash?' Anna said to Masha. 'How weird.'

'Yes,' said Masha.

'I wish Jackson had been here.' Anna sighed. 'But I wish he'd be at our last qualifiers tomorrow more.'

'Hmmmn,' was all Masha said, but Anna could tell by her tone that she thought so, too.

The A-, B- and C-teams were crammed three to a seat on the bus, ready to go to the first semifinal at Emu Downs School.

Emu Downs had only joined the chess competition that year, and when Phoenix had played them in an early qualifier they hadn't seemed so great. But as the season had progressed, they'd racked up more and more wins. Their A-team had been especially successful. Maybe they had some new players, or maybe they'd just been training hard. Whatever it was, the thought of playing them made Anna nervous, because Phoenix's A-team was in trouble. Mr F had put Olivia at number four, because of Jackson. She had tried to pull out because she didn't think she was good enough for the A-team semis, but Mr F he'd said she had to stay, or the A-team would forfeit. Olivia agreed, but she was miserable, and a miserable player never plays well.

Just before they left Phoenix, Mr F climbed out of the driver's seat and stood in the aisle. By the way he cleared his throat, the players knew they were in for a pep talk.

'Today's games are the most important of the season so far,' he said over the rattling of the bus's exhaust. 'And we're up against an unknown quantity. Don't be lulled into a false sense of security by what you remember of the Emu Downs players. Clearly, they have improved out of sight, or they wouldn't be in the semis.'

'Or they cheated,' someone grumbled.

'Yeah,' someone else said. 'I heard they put state players in as their reserves, and that's why they've won.'

There was a chorus of resentful mutterings, until Mr F put up his hand.

'Teams, I want you to go in and play the best

game you can, using everything you've learned. I ask no more of you than that.'

'Yes, sir.'

'Who said, "Methodical thinking is of more use in chess than inspiration"?'

'Don't know, sir,' they all said.

'Grandmaster Cecil Purdy,' Mr F said. 'You must take nothing for granted. Think before you move. And above all, move slowly.'

'Jackson's moving slowly already, sir,' one of the C-team piped up. 'Look!'

The kids all craned to see. Sure enough, there, on the other side of the oval, where some kids were playing soccer, was Jackson. He was walking as slowly as it was humanly possible to walk. But it looked as if he was walking towards the bus.

'Is he coming?' Anna said. 'Or is he just – wandering?'

Anna could only tell Jackson was walking at all because he put one foot in front of the other. He had his bag over his shoulder – a different bag to the one that someone had graffitied with yoghurt, Anna noticed – and he looked as if he were frowning.

Josh tugged on one of the bus windows. It was jammed, and it made a crunching sound as Josh pulled it open, bit by bit. He stuck his head out of the window and yelled, 'Jackson, Jackson!'

The other chess kids scrambled for the windows as well. Soon they were all calling, 'Jackson, Jackson!' Even Mr F joined in.

Jackson looked up. He began to smile, and after he smiled, he began to walk faster, and then to run. He ran past the soccer players, including Flash Buckley. Flash was about to kick the ball to Ben, but he paused while Jackson ran by, as if he expected Jackson to peel away and join the game. When he saw that Jackson was headed towards the chess bus, he kicked the ball away from the players and stormed off towards the classroom.

When Jackson reached the bus steps, he was puffing, pink-cheeked, and grinning from ear to ear.

The chess kids cheered louder than if he'd won Outstanding Athlete of the Year. Jackson looked more pleased than if he'd won Outstanding Athlete of the Year.

'Jackson!' Anna said, with delight and relief.

'Jackson!' Olivia said, with even more delight and relief.

'Sorry I'm late, sir,' Jackson said. He slid into the seat behind Anna and Masha.

'They're going to be a tough team, you know,' Anna said to Jackson.

'This could be a bad idea,' Jackson said.

'Then why'd you come?'

Jackson shrugged. 'I realised I wanted to. But . . .'

Anna raised her eyebrows.

'I mean, what if I lose, and that's it for the A-team? You'd really hate me more than Flash Buckley then.'

Anna thought for a while, and then grinned. 'I couldn't hate anyone more than Flash Buckley.'

' "Let's go fight on the ancient battle ground of the chessboard," ' Mr F bellowed. 'Who said that, squad?'

'Don't know, sir.'

'I did,' Mr F said, crunched the bus into gear, and drove to Emu Downs.

Emu Downs school was in a valley surrounded by tall trees, and as the Phoenix bus drove up to the gate, kangaroos leapt from where they'd been foraging at the side of the road and across the playing fields. But the tranquillity of their surroundings was contrasted by the determined and steely looks on the faces of the Emu Downs players.

Mr F usually had to quieten Josh and some of the others whenever they went to a new school, but this time nobody was making any noises.

'Good luck, Phoenix,' Mr F said. 'Take your positions.'

Anna's opponent was a boy who smiled politely for a microsecond before they drew lots for white, and then hunched over the board so far that the coaches both had to tell him to shift back several times during the game. He also moved deliberately slowly, but Anna used the time to examine every possible move she could make, and every consequence of every combination of every possible move that her opponent could make in return. She was concentrating so hard that when the time was up, they had only just started developing their pieces.

'Mr F,' Anna said, 'we haven't finished.'

'Who was going to win?'

'Me,' Anna said. 'I think.'

'No way,' said her opponent. 'See how I was positioning my bishops to pen in your king?'

'Yes, and you'll see that my knights were ready to attack you when you did.'

'But what about that?' the boy said, pointing at his attacking queen.

'Oh,' Anna said.

Mr F put up his hand.

'Wait,' he said. 'We'll collect the results from the other tables, and then we'll make an assessment.'

Anna and her opponent both crossed their arms and sat back in their chairs. Masha came over to Anna's board.

'Did you win?' Anna asked.

Masha nodded.

'Well done,' Anna said.

'Josh?'

Masha put her hand out to indicate stalemate – a draw.

'Jackson?'

Masha shook her head.

'How about the B-team? The C-team?'

Masha kept shaking her head.

'Oh,' Anna said.

Mr F was away with the other coach for a long time, recording the results, sorting out disputes. The other A-team players had gathered around, including Jackson, who stood hunched over, his hands jammed in his pockets.

Because Jackson had lost, it meant the A-team's place in the finals hinged on whether or not Anna would have won if they'd kept going.

Anna looked at the board again. She and her

opponent were exactly even in material, and Anna had been careful to make sure her king was well defended before she started attacking. But every time she tried to think ahead to what would happen in certain combinations, she could not imagine how the board would look.

'Right,' Mr F said. 'This is Mr Craig, the Emu Downs coach. Now, players, talk us through what you expect would have happened from here.'

Anna's opponent described what would have happened on the board as clearly as if he were seeing it in front of him. Anna stared, trying to imagine it as he talked.

'And then,' he said triumphantly, 'I would have had her in checkmate.'

Anna tried to work out whether what he was saying was right, but her mind had turned blurry.

Then a voice said, 'No, you wouldn't.'

Everyone turned to look at Jackson.

'She would have countered you with her rook two moves back, and you would have lost the bishop.'

The coaches looked at the board.

'That's exactly right,' Mr F said slowly. 'Do you agree, Mr Craig?'

'I'm afraid so,' Mr Craig said. 'And in five moves after that – '

'Stalemate,' Jackson said. 'It would have been a draw, like Josh's.'

'Yes,' Mr F said.

'Oh no,' Anna's opponent said.

'Good game,' Anna said.

Mr F shook Mr Craig's hand, and then pointed in the direction of the bus.

Anna sat silently next to Masha on the way home, staring out the window.

'Well, teams,' Mr F said before he started the bus, 'you all worked extremely hard today. Emu Downs was tough, but you all played slowly and thoughtfully, and that's the best you can ask for. B- and C-teams, you should be proud you've made it into the semis – next year it'll be the finals. A-team – you made it by a whisker, but a whisker is all it takes. So, well done. I hope you all feel proud of your achievements, no matter what your results were today.'

Back at school, Anna brooded in class and didn't even open her science book. She'd hoped Flash would say something to her, or to Jackson, so that she could turn around and be really mean to him, but he acted as if he hadn't noticed Masha, Jackson and Anna come in just before the bell went.

After class, Anna hung around the library until it was time for the librarian to lock up, and then she slung her bag over her shoulder and shuffled off towards her house. She knew that her mother would ask her to replay the game she'd played today, would suggest moves that Anna hadn't even thought of. Anna sighed, and walked slower.

As she made her way across the oval, she saw that she wasn't the only one who didn't want to go home.

21

Jackson was running – running and thinking.

He thought over the game he'd lost. It was the same problem he always had: after a strong opening and a well-positioned, sustained attack, Jackson blundered in the endgame. It was as if he couldn't work out what to do once the board opened up and he had to rely on individual pieces instead of the whole army of pawns, rooks, bishops and knights. He knew what he was supposed to do, but somehow his opponent always caught him by surprise.

He'd practised endgame tactics on the internet, and every time he lost in squad or on his Nintendo he tried to understand what had gone wrong.

Understanding wasn't enough, though. He had to translate it to a win. But against really good players he struggled.

He was on his fifth lap when he saw Anna.

'Hi,' Anna said.

'Hi,' Jackson puffed, coming to a stop.

'How come you're running?' Anna said. 'Flash is Outstanding Athlete of the Year – you don't have to train anymore.'

'Helps me think.'

Anna laughed. 'What, think about the hideous chess semi?'

Jackson glared at her, and then walked off.

'You're the one who got me to come,' he said over his shoulder. 'What a great idea that was!'

Anna jogged to catch up with him. 'Wait,' she said, puffing as much after a few steps as Jackson had after running for twenty minutes. 'I didn't mean you. I meant – all of us.'

Jackson stopped. 'The A-team did okay, as it turned out.'

'I was talking about my game, actually,' Anna said. 'At least you lost playing a state player.

They put him at number four so he wouldn't be so conspicuous. State players are only supposed to be reserves.'

Jackson's eyes widened. 'You're kidding.'

'Didn't Mr F tell you? So, you might have lost, but any of us would have lost, playing him.'

Jackson looked brighter for a moment, then sighed. 'Yeah, maybe, but I still made the same mistakes I always make. I just lose it in the endgame.'

'At least you know where you make mistakes,' Anna said. 'I just don't know what's wrong with me.'

'Generally, or with chess?'

'Don't be so rude,' Anna snapped.

'Don't be so sensitive,' Jackson said. 'I was only teasing.'

'Oh,' Anna said.

'You were saying?'

'What?' Anna said.

'About chess,' Jackson said in a slow voice.

Anna peered at him, then said, 'Well, the thing is, I get through the game, and I'm all right for the first while, but then it's like a fog comes over me, and nothing's clear.'

'That's why I run.' Jackson shrugged. 'Doesn't help me with my endgames, though.'

'I couldn't run,' Anna said.

'Why not?'

'I just – can't. Don't. Won't.'

'Not even if it helped you think?'

'It helps *you* think. It wouldn't help *me* think.'

'You don't know.'

'I don't run. I'm not running.'

'No, you're standing still.'

Anna punched Jackson on the arm. 'You know what I mean. I just want to win chess again. In the A-team. In the finals.'

'Me too.'

'More than anything.'

'Yep.'

They went silent, and then Jackson said, 'I've got an idea.'

'Put sneezing powder on their chairs, so we win by default?'

'Nope.'

'Hide a chess program under the desk?'

'Nuh-uh.'

'Get Josh to distract them so much they get demented and run away screaming?'

'We do a deal,' Jackson said. 'You help me with my endgames, and I'll help you.'

'How are you going to help me?' Anna asked suspiciously.

'You're going to run.'

'No, I'm not.'

'You want to win?'

'I want to win without running.'

'You're a chicken.'

'I am not!'

'So,' Jackson smiled, 'is it a deal?'

Anna looked at the sky for a moment, then back at Jackson. 'Maybe.'

Jackson put out his hand. Anna shook it.

'There's just one more thing,' Anna said. '*I* can't help you with your endgame, Jackson. But I know someone who can.'

'You have to realise that the value of the pieces changes at the end of the game,' Anna's mother was saying. 'Your pawns become stronger, and your king must come into play.'

'Okay,' Jackson said.

'Here is an endgame. White to move. What would you do?'

Jackson studied the board. 'The knight?'

Anna's mother moved the knight, and paused.

'Bad move.'

'Exactly.'

'Try again?'

When he pointed to the pawn, Anna's mother said, 'Think. If you do this, what will black do?'

Jackson rubbed the sides of his head with his hands. 'This is so hard.'

'No,' Anna's mother said. 'It is not hard. It is logic. It is seeing in your mind, seeing the consequences of each move for each player. You are like God, and you cannot err.'

Anna cringed, but Jackson didn't react. He stared at the board for a long time. Finally, he said, 'This is it.'

Instead of telling him whether he was right or not, Anna's mother merely played the next move. Again, Jackson frowned at the board for ages before he moved. Anna's mother moved; Jackson moved.

'Can you see now?'

Jackson's face was blank.

'No,' he said.

'Keep looking.'

He looked. His face was pinker than after he'd been running, and he seemed to barely blink. Finally, he looked up in amazement.

'Three moves to checkmate. I sacrifice the rook, and you're trapped.'

Anna's mother didn't smile. 'I'll see you tomorrow,' she said, and got up. 'I have to work now.'

'So, did I get it?' Jackson was confused. He looked over at Anna, but Anna was busy putting the pieces away. 'I got it, didn't I, Mrs P?'

'You let opinions crowd in,' Anna's mother said. 'You must just look, and play.'

Anna's mother disappeared down the passageway.

'Mum won't tell you something you already know,' Anna said. 'But she'll always tell you when you're wrong.'

'She's scary,' Jackson said. Anna looked up sharply, and he added, 'But amazing.'

'Do you want to come back?'

'Yeah,' he said, 'if my brain stops hurting.'

'She was going easy.' Anna grinned. 'Just you wait.'

'Just *you* wait,' Jackson said, 'until we start running. Tomorrow.'

Anna clutched her stomach. 'I may become seriously ill.'

'The day after.'

'Ow,' she said. 'Did I mention I've broken my toe?'

'You are going,' Jackson said, 'to run.'

'Away,' Anna said. 'Only away.'

'You want to win, or what?'

'Losing seems less painful than running.'

Jackson raised one eyebrow.

'Okay,' Anna said. 'I'll be there. But if anyone sees me, I'm never running again.'

'I think you're safe.'

'You'd better be right.'

'You'd better turn up.'

'I don't have a choice.'

'No,' Jackson said. 'You don't.'

'I'm dying,' Anna moaned. 'My lungs hurt.'

'They need to get used to it,' said Jackson. 'You need to get used to it.'

'But lungs aren't supposed to hurt. Lungs are supposed to take in air. Air isn't supposed to hurt.' Anna bent double and moaned again. 'Ohhhh.'

'Stop complaining,' Jackson said. 'Once you get your breath back, you're going again.'

'No,' Anna said. 'It's torture.'

'It's exercise.'

'Same difference.'

'Off you go. It's only a hundred metres.'

'It's too far.'

'Go!'

Anna ran. Even though the grass was flat, it seemed uneven, and she didn't feel as if she was running so much as stumbling.

'Run as if you're gliding over the grass!' Jackson yelled at her.

'I feel like an elephant!' Anna yelled back. 'Elephants don't glide.'

'And don't forget to breathe,' Jackson yelled. 'Slow, even breaths.'

'How can I breathe slowly when I'm dying?'

'You're not dying, you're running.'

'Same thing.'

'Stop arguing and run!'

When Anna had made it to the end of the track, Jackson ran to catch up. Anna had collapsed and was lying on the grass.

'Better,' Jackson said.

'Don't lie,' Anna said. 'I'm practically dead now.' She felt her pulse. 'My heart is about to explode.'

'Get up,' Jackson said. 'One more time and we'll be done for today. Tomorrow you can run a whole lap.'

'Tomorrow I will be a corpse,' Anna said.

'One more time,' Jackson said. 'Then we're going to your house for endgame practice.'

Anna staggered to her feet, and back down the track again. She was almost at the end when she suddenly stopped.

'Anna!' Jackson jogged towards her.

Flash Buckley. Flash Buckley had been behind one of the trees, and now he came wandering in their direction.

'What do you want, Flash?' Anna said, her voice hard.

Flash didn't say anything straight away. Anna glared at him some more.

'I want to talk to Jackson,' Flash said. 'Alone.'

Jackson arrived, and stood next to Anna.

'Why would I want to talk to you?' Jackson said, crossing his arms.

Flash looked at the ground, scuffed his toe on the grass. 'I wanted to say sorry,' he mumbled.

'What for?'

'You know,' Flash said. 'The yoghurt. Being mean.'

'That was you?' Anna said. 'I should have known.'

'Well, you got what you wanted,' Jackson said. 'Congratulations on Outstanding Athlete. Good work.'

'That's just it,' Flash said. 'I haven't taken it.'

'You won,' Jackson said.

'I haven't won,' Flash said.

'I didn't want you to win,' Anna pointed out. 'I was barracking for Chelsea.'

'Why don't you just run away?' Flash turned on Anna. 'If you can run, that is.'

'Listen, you – ' Anna began, but Jackson interrupted.

'If you want to say anything, say it now. Or go away.'

'All right then,' Flash said. 'It's like this. I've talked to Ms S, and she's agreed.'

'Agreed to what?'

'Another cross-country race. Week after next.'

'We already did cross-country.'

'You didn't swim,' Flash said.

'You told the coach about chess.'

'Yeah, but – ' Flash stepped from foot to foot, and looked at the ground again.

'And dumping the yoghurt, and all that – what did you think I was going to do?'

'I thought you were going to give up chess!' Flash said.

Jackson blinked for a moment. Then he said, 'What difference does it make? You should be pleased.'

Flash was quiet for a while, then he said, 'If I don't beat you it doesn't mean anything.'

Jackson shook his head. 'I don't know. I've got to focus on the chess finals.'

'Just think about it,' Flash said.

'All right,' Jackson nodded.

Flash put out his hand to Jackson. Jackson paused for a long time before he shook it.

Flash smiled – a real smile – and then ran off.

'Are you going to do it?' said Anna.

Jackson shrugged. 'I don't care about running. I care about chess.'

'Same here,' Anna said. 'But you're making me run.'

'That's different.'

'I'd love to see you beat him. So would the whole school.'

'I wish I was as good at chess as I am at running. Running's easy.'

'Chess is easy. Compared to running.'

Jackson shrugged again.

'At least he didn't laugh at me,' said Anna.

'Yeah,' said Jackson.

'I wonder if he'll tell everyone at school.'

'Maybe.'

'I think I preferred him when he was foul.'

'Definitely.'

'Can we go home now?'

'Good try. You've still got to do your hundred metres. Go!'

'Good play, Jackson,' Mr F said. 'You've really picked up your endgame. You beat me fair and square.'

'Thanks, sir.' Jackson grinned.

'Who said, "Openings teach you openings. End-games teach you chess!"?' Mr F said, standing up.

'Don't know, sir,' mumbled the players.

'Chess master Stephan . . . Stephan . . . with the name starting with G?' said Jackson.

'Gerzadowicz,' Mr F said. 'Exactly right. And you, Jackson, are learning chess.'

Mr F wandered around the chess room, and stopped at Anna and Masha's game.

'Well played, Anna,' Mr F said. 'You've been surpassing yourself lately.'

'Thanks, sir,' Anna said. 'I've been running.'

Masha stared at Anna.

'It helps my concentration,' Anna said, but Masha kept staring.

'It certainly does,' Mr F said. 'Who said, "Your body has to be in top condition. Your chess deteriorates as your body does. You can't separate body from mind"?'

'Grandmaster Bobby Fischer,' Anna said. 'Even I know that.'

'That's right,' Mr F said. 'Chess is a sport.'

'No way,' Anna said.

'Yeah,' Jackson said. 'It's not like you raise a sweat or anything. Most of the time.'

'Think about it,' Mr F said. 'You have two teams – two players – competing against each other to win. Of course it's a sport.'

'But sir,' Jackson said, 'you need to use your muscles for it to be sport. Don't you?'

'You need endurance, discipline, and toughness to be a good chess player – mental muscle,' Mr F said.

'Oh,' said Anna. Then she laughed. 'Hey. I play a *sport*. Wait till I tell Flash Buckley.'

'Nobody else thinks of it as a sport,' said Jackson. 'Obviously.'

'If it's a sport, the whole school should come and watch the finals,' said Anna.

'But most kids don't know how to play,' Olivia said.

'We could teach them the moves, easy,' Anna said. 'All they need to know is how the pieces move, that's all. And about checkmate.'

The chess room became quiet as the players thought about what it would be like, playing chess in front of the whole school.

'Let's do it, sir,' Anna said. 'The squad members could go to different classrooms between now and the finals, and teach everyone how to play.'

'I suppose you could,' Mr F said. 'But how would everyone be able to see?'

'You could set up screens for some of the games,' said Olivia.

'You could,' Mr F nodded. 'But the school would have to agree to all this. That might be a bit tricky.'

And then Jackson had an idea. It was such a good idea that his hand shot straight in the air.

But when Mr F said, 'What is it, Jackson?', Jackson shook his head.

It wasn't Mr F he needed to speak to.

It was Flash Buckley.

Jackson was running. This time, he wasn't running for the sake of it. He wasn't running just because it was what he'd always done, or just because he wanted to beat Flash Buckley – although beating Flash Buckley was exactly what he needed to do.

He was running for chess.

'This is the race that will determine who is Outstanding Athlete of the Year,' Ms S had bellowed through the loudspeaker. 'We also have special prizes for the winner of each year group, and Outstanding Effort awards. So Phoenix competitors, please take your marks, get set . . .'

Flash Buckley had been at his heel from the moment Ms S fired the starter gun. Jackson was surprised, because normally Jackson's long legs and quick reflexes gave him the advantage at the beginning of a race. Not this time. This time, Flash was determined not to let Jackson get away from him. This time, Flash meant business. He must have been training hard to have improved his take-off like that.

But this time, Jackson meant business too.

Usually, with cross-country, Jackson got into a rhythm, his strides long and even and strong, breathing in for two paces, out for two, the wind cooling him as he went. But today he was so aware of Flash, right there, waiting to overtake, waiting for Jackson to stumble or slow, that he couldn't find a comfortable timing. He was going too fast for that; he was sprinting, even though he knew that you shouldn't sprint for long distances. If you sprinted early on, you got tired. And if you got tired, you slowed down.

Jackson didn't see how he could stop sprinting, because he worried that if Flash got ahead of him, even for a moment, he'd never catch up. Jackson had been running to think, running to help Anna think, but it wasn't the same as the training that Flash must have been doing. So he needed to stay even with Flash. Didn't he?

Jackson's muscles started burning, and his throat and lungs ached. This isn't good, Jackson thought. This was the way you were supposed to feel at the end of a race, not the beginning. He was running too fast.

They ran past the junior oval, where the houses were in their roped-off areas, each waving their flags and cheering. All of the junior school was there, and so were the kids from the senior school who weren't running. When they saw Flash and Jackson emerge from the thicket of trees, they began chanting.

'Jackson.'

'Flash Buckley.'

'Jackson.'

'Flash Buckley.'

Jackson produced a grin that felt more like a grimace, and the wind made his lips dry to his teeth. He felt Flash surge forward, and so he surged too. The kids cheered louder. Jackson knew most of the chess squad was there, barracking for him, no matter what house they were in. But Flash was still visible, his blue T-shirt bright in the corner of Jackson's eye. Was it his imagination, or was Flash closer than he had been before?

Jackson thought, I'm getting tired. I'm going to lose.

Then he thought about chess.

He thought about the importance of the end-game, and how all of your moves had to be means to the final checkmate. If your first strategy didn't work, you tried another.

As Flash streaked ahead of him, he could almost feel Flash's shock, and his confidence.

Flash thought he'd won now that Jackson was exhausted. He ran ahead, confident that the Outstanding Athlete of the Year award was his. There were two laps to go, only two laps, and the trophy and the triumph would belong to him. Flash Buckley was going to be Outstanding Athlete of the Year, at last. And this time, he was going to win it fair and square, against Jackson.

Jackson watched Flash go.

'You don't have to this time, Anna,' Ms S said. 'Most of the chess kids aren't.'

'I want to,' Anna said.

'All right,' Ms S said. 'But I don't want the whole school to have to wait for you. It's not fair for everyone else.'

'You won't have to,' Anna said. 'I promise.'

Anna placed herself in the middle of the cross-country runners, who looked sideways at her. Anna, chess nut, looked as if she was actually preparing to race. Anna ignored the glances, and craned her neck so she could see the front of the pack. There was Chelsea, stretching her arms this way and that, as if she was about to swim rather than run. There was

Flash Buckley, jogging on the spot, as if he couldn't wait. But where was Jackson? Maybe he'd changed his mind, after all. But then she saw him, looking as serious as if he were about to start a chess game, absolutely still, facing forward.

Go, Jackson! Anna said to herself.

'This is the race that will determine who is Outstanding Athlete of the Year,' Anna heard Ms S say through the loudspeaker, her voice tinny and high. 'We also have special prizes for the winner of each group, and Outstanding Effort awards. So Phoenix competitors, please take your marks, get set . . .'

For the first time ever, Anna actually tried to take off with the other racers, pushing against the ground, leaping forward. It felt strange, running with other kids. It wasn't the same as running alone on the oval with Jackson, where the only thing she had to worry about was how to get to the end of the hundred metres, or the end of the lap, or, as Jackson had made her practise this week, the end of three laps. It seemed to her that lots of the runners were going really slowly. She almost tripped on the heels of Nelson, in front of her, and after she'd passed him, she had to weave around Gabi and Shenae. Gabi and Shenae were both usually sporty and fast, and Anna wondered why they weren't further ahead. Then she remembered Jackson saying that in cross-country you shouldn't go too fast or you'd get a stitch and have to stop. You had to be steady and even, get your pace right, and relax into the running.

Jackson was right, Anna thought. After a while, there weren't so many kids in front of her, and she could almost pretend she was alone on the track. She thought about the chess finals next week. They were playing Condor South again, and this time the Phoenix team was prepared. Anna hoped she would be number one, so she could face Sophie again, and prove that she, Anna, was the better player. She was going to keep her mind on the game, not be distracted, not be nervous.

Before she knew it, Anna was on her last lap. Jackson hadn't lapped her, so she knew she must have been going fast enough to keep up with most of the runners. In fact, she was sure that she'd lapped some of the younger kids. But now she was growing tired, and her body felt as if it was getting heavier and heavier with each step.

Anna heard voices yelling. It must be the crowd calling for Jackson and Flash, she thought.

They yelled, 'Jackson!'

'Flash Buckley!'

'Jackson!'

'Flash Buckley!'

Surely they couldn't have tied – again?

Anna became aware of somebody coming up behind her. She turned around, and saw it was Ben, one of Flash's friends.

'Out of my way,' Ben huffed.

'Don't tell me what to do,' Anna huffed back.

She didn't think she had any energy left. Her muscles felt weak from the exertion, her lungs were burning, and part of her wanted to collapse on the ground and catch her breath. But somehow, with Ben drawing close, she was able to make her legs go faster, to push past the weakness and keep going.

'I said, out of my way,' Ben hissed.

This time, Anna couldn't waste any breath

replying. She heard his feet striking the ground, and saw his arms jerking back and forth out of the corner of her eye. She had to keep going, had to.

The thicket of trees suddenly ended, and there was the finish line. She was puffing and heaving, but she commanded herself to go faster.

When the crowd saw her and Ben racing, they yelled and cheered. Anna smiled, and the wind dried her lips and stuck her smile to her teeth. Ben was beside her, and Anna knew she had one last chance.

She forced one extra surge of energy into her limbs, and sprinted to the finish line, leaving Ben behind her.

The crowd cheered and called. Anna skidded onto the ground, and put her head on her knees. She was so exhausted and dizzy she wondered if she was going to be sick. It seemed to be a long time before she could stop gasping for breath.

'Good race,' she said to Ben, when she was able. Ben looked as if he were in more pain than she was.

'Huh,' Ben said. 'I didn't know you could run.'

'Neither did I,' Anna said. Then she looked

around. There was Jackson, and Chelsea, and Flash Buckley standing around ahead, and kids were starting to cross the line behind her. 'Where is everyone else? And who won?' she asked Ben.

But Ben had got up and was walking towards Flash. So Anna turned and looked at the spectators for the first time. And got a huge surprise.

Masha, Olivia and Josh were standing in front of everyone, holding up a banner. The banner was long and white, and on it, in big black letters, were the words:

Anna is our number one.

Anna wondered if she were seeing things, so she blinked hard, once, twice, three times. When they saw her, Masha, Olivia and Josh lifted up the banner and waved it.

Anna climbed to her feet and jogged over to Masha, Olivia and Josh, and said, 'Thanks, guys.'

Josh grunted and grinned; Masha just looked pleased.

'It was Masha's idea,' Olivia said. 'She told us – '

'Told you?' Anna said, puzzled.

'Yeah,' Olivia said.

Masha cleared her throat, and said, 'I thought, if Anna will try to run, maybe Masha will try to speak.'

Anna's jaw was loose with shock, and Masha smiled.

'It's okay, Anna,' Masha said. 'I'll never talk as much as you.'

'Nobody could talk as much as you,' Olivia added.

'I always thought you could understand more than what you let on,' said Anna.

'Yes.'

'Even Mr F's sayings?'

'Yes.'

'Flash Buckley calling us names?'

'Yes.'

'What about my insults?'

'Definitely. They're great.'

'Stupendous,' Anna said.

Olivia poked Anna in the ribs, and pointed up at the podium. Flash, Chelsea and Jackson were all there, plus one or two of the younger kids.

'Quick,' Olivia said to Anna. 'Get up there. Ms S is waving you over.'

Anna had never seen Ms S smile at her, but she was smiling now.

'And so,' she said into the microphone, 'it gives me great pleasure to give the Outstanding Effort Award to . . . Anna!'

Ms S looped a ribbon around her neck with a big gold medal dangling on it.

'Congratulations, Anna,' she said. 'I'm sure we've never had a competitor come last in one race, and fourth the next. An outstanding effort.'

'Really?' Anna said, shaking Ms S's hand. 'I came fourth?'

'You're the second girl, after Chelsea,' Ms S said.

'But Ms S,' Anna said, 'that can't be right. You must have mixed me up with someone else.'

'No, Anna, it's right, all right.'

'But, miss, I'm terrible at sport.'

'Maybe you're not fast in sprints,' Ms S said, 'but you've got endurance.' Ms S tapped her forehead. 'Must be all the concentration for chess.'

She turned back to the crowd and said, 'And now, the best runner in year four . . .'

Anna stood there on the podium, tingling with surprise. She, Anna, had a medal. A sports medal. If it hadn't been for Jackson, she never would have known she could run.

She looked around for Jackson. He was standing to the side with Flash and Chelsea, and Anna couldn't tell from looking at them who had won. Flash looked annoyed, Chelsea looked comfortable and confident, the way she always did, and Jackson was standing almost as still as he had been at the beginning of the race. Anna couldn't work out whether he looked pleased, disappointed, or something else altogether.

'Jackson!' Anna hissed. But Jackson didn't hear

her, and kept staring ahead. She hoped he'd won, but she just wasn't sure.

More awards were called and athletes congratulated. Anna was getting hot, standing in the sun, and it felt like forever before Ms S said, 'Now, Phoenix school, it is time for the final announcement of the place-getters in today's race.'

The crowd produced a brief round of applause, then quietened.

'In third place is our winning girl, Chelsea!'

Chelsea's house sang their song as Chelsea leaned over so Ms S could slip the ribbon over her head. Chelsea stood next to Anna in the line of winners.

'Congratulations,' Chelsea said. 'You can really run.'

'Thanks. Do you know who won?'

Chelsea shook her head. 'It looked like they drew.'

'Again?'

'That's what everyone reckons.'

Anna expected that Ms S would get on with announcing who got second place, but instead, she decided to make a speech. Anna wanted to roll her eyes, but she didn't want the whole school to see, so she pressed her lips together and tried not to look impatient.

'It's not often a school produces two outstanding athletes from the same year,' Ms S was saying. 'But that's exactly what we've done here at Phoenix school. In all of their competitions, Flash Buckley and Jackson have been neck-and-neck, sometimes Jackson inching ahead, sometimes Flash. Jackson has managed to be Outstanding Athlete of the Year for the past two years, but he's only managed it with Flash Buckley right at his heels.'

'That's because Jackson wants to get away from him,' muttered Anna.

'But this year, we saw something different. Flash Buckley won Outstanding Athlete of the Year fair and square. However, he demonstrated the heights of sportsmanship when he elected to have a rematch – to make sure that the rivalry was kept alive, to make sure that we, Phoenix school, were here to witness a competition between equals.'

'Get me a bucket,' Anna said.

'Shhh,' Chelsea hissed.

'Before I announce the winner not only of this race, but of the honour that is Outstanding Athlete of the Year, I want to say that you are both outstanding sportspeople, and you have done your school proud.'

Anna rolled her eyes. The rest of the school clapped and whistled and waved their house flags.

'It gives me great pleasure to announce that the Outstanding Athlete of the Year is . . .'

Anna stopped rolling her eyes and leaned forward. 'Please let it be Jackson,' she whispered.

'Flash Buckley!'

Anna felt as if she'd been kicked in the stomach. She glanced at Jackson, who still looked as if he hadn't moved. She expected that Jackson would be devastated, to have agreed to the rematch only to have lost. It made it seem as if Flash Buckley had won not only the race, but a personal victory over Jackson. As if he had laid a kind of trap that Jackson had stepped into.

But Jackson didn't look disappointed at all. For the first time, he was smiling. And he was joining in with the applause as if he meant it.

Flash Buckley accepted the medal from Ms S, then held it up to the school. A roar rose from the crowd, and Flash stood there, his arms above his head, held wide, the way politicians do when they win elections. But then he walked up to the microphone.

'What's he doing?' Anna said.

'Making a speech, I guess,' Chelsea said.

'But Flash never makes speeches. He – '

'Shhh,' Chelsea hissed.

Flash cleared his throat. 'Thanks everyone,' he said. 'This is really good. It's awesome. Thanks.'

Everyone applauded the way they did when a speech was finished. But Flash didn't move. He stood there until the crowd settled down, and said, 'But as Outstanding Athlete of the Year, I have something I am asking you all to do.'

'Huh?' Chelsea said.

'We play sport, and we have our competitions. But there's one sport that Phoenix school plays that nobody knows about. I mean, that nobody watches. And it's about time we did.'

Anna shot Jackson a look. This time, Jackson saw her looking, and winked.

'Phoenix is about to be in the finals of that sport, right here at this school. And that sport is chess.'

Anna could see kids looking at each other, and saying, '*What*?'

'So next week, the chess players are going to come to your classes and they're going to teach you how to play chess. And then the entire school is going to come to the Chess Championships, and we're going to support our players so that they can win.'

'You're kidding me,' Chelsea said. 'Chess?'

'That's all,' Flash said. 'Thank you.'

This time, Anna stared at Jackson, and Jackson gave her a smile of pure happiness straight back.

'I can't believe it,' Anna said.

'Neither can I,' grumbled Chelsea. 'How weird. Why would the rest of us want to watch something as boring as that?'

Anna wanted to say something mean. Instead, she took a breath and said, 'Chelsea, do you know how to play chess?'

'Of course not,' Chelsea said. 'We're not all brainiacs like you, Anna.'

'It's a sport, like Flash said. Just wait till we show you. Bye.' And Anna skipped off to join Jackson, her medal bouncing as she ran.

'And Jackson had worked it out with Ms S, but then he had to convince Flash Buckley to do it,' Anna told her father as he stirred pasta sauce. 'He was worried that Flash wouldn't, but Flash was so glad that Jackson had raced him that he did it.' Anna jiggled on her chair and said, 'So everyone's going to watch the finals. The whole school.'

'That's great, sweetheart,' her father said.

'Don't jiggle the table,' her mother said, bending over her laptop.

'Sorry, Mum,' Anna said.

'And you've got a medal,' Anna's father added. 'That's really something. Isn't that something, Del?'

'Yes,' her mother said, her eyes on the screen.

'So now we've got to think about how to explain to the other classes how to play chess,' Anna said. 'Just the basics, like how the pieces get taken, and checkmate.'

Now her mother looked up.

'I don't understand how you are expected to concentrate with so many children there,' Anna's mother said. 'They will not sit still. They will not understand. And they will distract you.'

'I'm sure they'll be on their best behaviour,' Anna's father said.

'Thanks, Dad,' Anna said. Her mother was frowning at her.

'Chess is not a sport,' Anna's mother said. 'It is a game of seriousness and concentration.'

'We'll feel good having everyone there,' Anna said. 'People play better when what they're doing matters.'

'This shouldn't apply to chess,' her mother said. 'I'll email the school with my objections.'

'Del,' Anna's father said, 'there's no need for that.'

'It makes an important thing trivial,' Anna's mother said. 'I'll send it straight away.'

'Don't you dare!' Anna cried. 'We want this. Everyone wants this.'

'What harm can it do?' Anna's father said.

'Anna can become a very good chess player, now she has improved her concentration,' Anna's mother said. 'I don't see what benefit this can bring.'

'I like it,' Anna said. 'I like people caring about what happens with the chess team. Everyone's always ignored us, or made fun of us, and now, because of Jackson, they're not. Don't try to ruin it, Mum.'

'That's not my intention. My intention is to make things correct.'

'Oh, what would you know?' Anna said. 'You don't understand – you don't care at all. I wish you weren't my mother!'

Anna rushed off to her room, slamming the door so hard the glass rattled in the pane.

Anna's father turned off the flame under the pasta sauce, and sighed.

'She can't see reason,' Anna's mother said.

'Sometimes,' Anna's father said, 'reason isn't everything.'

'How'd you go today?' Jackson's mother asked over dinner.

Jackson shrugged. 'Flash beat me.'

'Oh,' his mother said. She examined Jackson's face. 'You don't seem upset.'

'I'm not,' Jackson said. 'I did a deal with him. He's got the whole school coming to the chess finals.'

Jackson's mum said sharply, 'You didn't let him win, did you?'

'No,' Jackson said.

'Well. That's all right then.'

Jackson finished chewing a piece of lamb, and said, 'Mum, what's wrong with Dad?'

Jackson's mum blinked, and didn't seem to know what to say.

'I mean, I get it about the accident,' Jackson said. 'But how come he's not fixing up?'

Jackson's mum took a long breath in, and as she breathed out she seemed to sag.

'He is fixed up, Jackson,' she said. 'At least, his body's fixed, mostly.'

'I don't understand. Why does he stay in bed all day, then?'

Jackson's mum shook her head. 'He just . . . He just doesn't want to do anything anymore. Can't make himself want to. Jackson, your father lost his job and his mate in that accident. The world isn't the same for him anymore.'

'But there's not that much wrong with Dad,' Jackson said. 'I mean, he still uses a crutch and everything, but he's mostly okay. Isn't he?'

'He's still in a bit of pain,' his mother said. 'And he's still tired.'

'Would he come and watch me play in the finals?'

'Jackson,' she started, 'He – '

'It's okay,' Jackson said. 'I was just asking.'

'One day, I promise.'

'I said, it's okay,' Jackson snapped.

'Keep your voice down,' his mother said.

'I always do.' Jackson stood up from the table, got his plate and put it on the sink.

'Where are you going?' his mother asked.

'To my room,' he said. 'I've got to practise.'

She watched him go down the passageway and heard his door slam – hard.

Jackson, Anna and Masha took turns going to classes, explaining about chess. Josh came too, but he didn't say anything. Sometimes, kids who hadn't even been to chess practice thought they could play, and they put up their hands confidently when Jackson, Anna or Masha asked if anyone knew the moves. After Josh had demolished them, they became silent, and everyone listened when the A-team players tried to show them how to play properly.

'Chess is about war,' Anna explained.

'I thought it was a sport,' someone commented.

'Yeah,' someone else piped up. 'Nobody gets killed, do they?'

'That's what taken pawns and pieces are,' Anna said. 'It's like they've been killed.'

'So what's with the pawn at the end becoming a queen?'

'Like reincarnation.'

'Whooo-hoo, the queen back from the dead.'

'Whooo-hoo, she's come to get you – watch out!'

'Aggh! I've been killed by the ghost queen! Aggh!'

Then the boys started making gargling noises until the teacher asked them to be quiet.

'Maybe my mum was right,' Anna said to Jackson after they had tried to teach the year fives. 'Most of the kids can't even sit still long enough to remember which way a pawn moves. Maybe we should have chess players only there.'

'Yeah,' Jackson said.

'It was your idea.'

'I know.'

'We could lose. In front of everyone.'

'If I lose in front of everyone, it means I've lost at everything. In front of everyone.'

'"You learn much more from a game you lose than from a game you win,"' Anna said. 'Grandmaster Capoblanca said that.'

'Do you think that's true?'

'I don't know.'

'I hope we don't have to find out.'

For the week before the chess competition, Anna couldn't relax. She went running, but even that wasn't enough to tire her out properly.

'What's wrong?' said Masha one lunchtime.

'I don't know,' said Anna. 'I just feel weird.'

'Do you feel bad about me being number one?'

Anna looked at Masha. 'To be honest, I did.'

'I know,' Masha said. 'And you've been beating me a lot lately.'

'Actually, I'm more worried about that horrible Sophie seeing I've been demoted.' Anna sighed. 'She'll gloat.'

'I'm worried about playing her,' Masha said.

'But it's not just that.'

'What is it?'

'This is going to sound stupid.'

'You never sound stupid,' Masha said in a serious voice.

Just then, two year-five girls walked by and said, 'Hi Anna. Hi Masha', and continued on their way to the canteen.

'See?' Anna said. 'That's what I'm worried about.'

'What?'

'They never used to say anything to me.'

Masha looked puzzled.

Anna leaned forward, and continued, 'Lately everyone's been nice. I never used to care about whether people were nice or not.'

'And now you do?'

'Yes! But what if I lose in the Chess Championships – in front of everyone?'

'Hmmmn,' said Masha. Then, after a while she added, 'You have changed.'

'Have I?' Anna said. 'Is that good?'

Masha smiled. 'I think so.'

Anna sighed. 'Changed or not, I still feel nervous.'

The A-team were at school extra early on the day of the finals. It was a beautiful spring morning, with birds calling to each other from high in the trees, and a breeze that smelt of warm grass and sunshine. But the A-team didn't notice any of it. They were too busy trying to make sure that when Condor South arrived, all of the screens were set up, all the cameras were pointing the right way, and all of the school was assembled – quietly – on the stands in the undercover area.

'I feel sick,' Anna said to Mr F.

'It's just nerves,' Mr F said.

'Just?'

'Use them to focus your concentration.'

'That's the problem. How can I concentrate when I'm so nervous?'

Mr F paused, then said, 'That's exactly what your mother was concerned about.'

Anna was so shocked that for a moment she forgot to be nervous. 'She really did complain? She said she was going to.'

'Oh, yes.' Mr F smiled. 'She complained in some detail. Actually, there's something I needed to let you know, before we start,' Mr F began, but then he was distracted by Jackson and Josh carrying the tables from C4 to the undercover area. He yelled at them, 'Thanks, boys. Remember they need to all be in two lines, and put as much space between them as possible. Okay?'

'But Mr F,' Anna said, tugging his sleeve to get his attention, 'we're still playing, right? Even with Mum complaining.'

'Let's just say, we've come to an arrangement. Hang on, I'd better sort this out.' Mr F jogged off towards the boys to show them exactly what needed to go where.

By the time the Phoenix spectators began to

fill the stands, just before lunchtime, the tables were all in place, the boards were all ready, and the computers and screens were hooked up and tested. The players would each have a screen, and at the bottom of the screen was a display showing how many pieces each player had taken.

'This match is going to be the longest hour of our lives,' Anna said to Jackson.

When Jackson didn't reply, Anna said, 'Are you okay?'

'I don't feel good,' Jackson said.

'It's just nerves,' said Anna.

'Just?'

Anna laughed. Jackson frowned.

'I know,' Anna said. 'But remember. If it all goes wrong, it was your idea.'

'Thanks.'

'Any time.'

'I'm going to have one last run around the school. Sure you don't want to come?'

'Sure,' Anna said. 'Off you go.'

Anna wandered around the undercover area, trying to calm herself down. Some of the kids in the stands waved to her excitedly, and she waved back. Our school wants us to win, she thought. They're all behind us.

'Oh, Anna,' Mr F said, emerging from behind one of the projection screens as she wandered by. 'I'd better tell you about those couple of things now.'

Anna eyed him suspiciously. 'What?'

'First, you're number one today.'

For once, Anna couldn't think of anything to say.

'It's not just because you're playing well,' Mr F said, 'although you are. It's that Condor South are insisting that we have the same players in the same order. So you'll be playing Sophie, like you did last time.'

Anna swallowed. She didn't know whether to be delighted or terrified. She'd wanted to have another chance at beating Sophie, but that was when she didn't think she'd ever get another chance.

'Oh,' Anna squeaked. 'That's – great. I think.'

'Masha's relieved, actually,' Mr F said. 'She hated the idea of playing Sophie.'

'I know,' Anna said. 'Sophie's a chess machine.'

Anna turned to find Masha, so she could check that it really was okay with her. But then something – someone – caught her eye.

'Mr F,' Anna said in a low, quiet voice. 'What's my mother doing here?'

Mr F turned to where Anna's mother was bending over the computer, peering at the screen and tapping the keys.

'Oh, yes, the second thing,' Mr F said. 'There she is.'

'Your mother is going to be helping us,' Mr F said. 'We need an adjudicator in case there's a disagreement about the results. Condor South will have the same.'

'Why can't you do it, the way you normally do?'

'Because it's the finals. And I don't need to tell you the heightened feelings, let's say, that go along with finals.'

'But – there must be someone else.'

'Well, your mother obviously is a skilled player,' Mr F said. 'And she understands all the protocols.'

'But – but – '

As she was working out how she might be able to hide the fact that her mother was her mother,

Anna heard Jackson call out, 'Hey, Dr P! How come you're here?'

When Anna's mother saw Jackson coming, she produced a smile.

'You'll try out your endgame in competition,' she said to Jackson. 'We'll see how much you remember from our lessons.'

'I'll remember, don't you worry,' said Jackson.

'Ah, Anna,' Anna's mother said. 'Are you prepared for your match?' She glanced at her watch. 'Only fifteen minutes to go.'

'As prepared as I'm going to get,' Anna said miserably. 'Mum, have you met Mr F?'

'Only by email,' Mr F said, and put out his hand. Anna's mother pretended she hadn't seen the gesture, and turned back to the computer screen.

'I still think an audience is a distraction,' Anna's mother said, nodding at the filling stands. 'But I see the school is determined to do it. I take it they will become quiet when the match starts.'

'Don't worry,' Mr F said. 'They'll be as quiet as Deep Blue when it was playing Kasparov in 1997.'

'Mum,' Anna said, smiling through clenched teeth. 'Where's Dad?'

Anna's father helped Anna's mother seem less weird in public, but Anna's mother said, 'He's coming after the match. He had to work at the last minute.'

'Why didn't you tell me you were coming?'

'You didn't need anything to spoil your preparation,' Anna's mother said.

Outstanding, Anna thought. Just spoil the day instead.

'It's great you're able to help out, Del,' Mr F said. 'We really appreciate it.'

'Uh oh,' Jackson said, pointing. 'Here come Condor South.'

Anna was amazed at how quickly one person could change – for the worse.

Last time, Sophie was confident and unpleasant. This time, she was confident and rude.

'Oh, you again,' she said, when she saw Anna. And then she produced a cold smile. 'I hope you're planning on giving me a challenge this time.'

Anna had the urge to string together all the insulting words she'd ever called Flash and use them on Sophie. Instead, she took a deep breath. She knew that Sophie wanted to unsettle her, and she had to pretend she wasn't unsettled in the least.

'Welcome to Phoenix,' Anna said as pleasantly as she could manage. 'Good luck.'

Sophie looked around at all the Phoenix kids and said, 'Our school didn't need to come to support us. They know we'll ace you, the way we've been acing everyone this year.'

Anna swallowed. 'You haven't lost at all?'

'Not once,' Sophie said.

Anna pointed to the tables where the A-team would sit. Sophie went and placed herself at the number one table, even though there were a few minutes to go.

Anna went to find Jackson, to tell him how horrible Sophie was, but he was standing with two people who Anna guessed were his parents. His mum was smiling, and his dad was standing, holding himself up with a crutch under one arm, the other arm tight around Jackson. His dad had the kind of look that people get at airports when they meet up with family they haven't seen for a long time, half pleased and half looking as if they're about to cry. Jackson looked straight-out pleased. Until Mr F's voice came booming through the microphone.

'Spectators, teachers, parents, visitors from

175

Condor South – please take your seats,' he said. 'The Grand Final of the Statewide Chess Tournaments is about to begin.'

Anna took a deep breath, and one last look around the stands. The school was all there, everyone in their houses, just like they had been for the sports championships. And then she saw Flash Buckley and one of his friends stand up. They bent over, and Anna wondered, with a stab, what awful thing they had planned. She wondered if they were going to throw stink bombs at the players, the way Flash and his friends did once in year three at assembly, or if they were going to turn around and bare their bottoms, the way they did on the last day of school in year four.

Then Anna saw what it was they were doing. They were unfurling a huge banner, even huger than the one Masha had made for Anna at the cross-country. What insulting thing was it going to say? Anna looked over at Jackson, who had stopped halfway towards his table. Jackson was staring as well, and Anna could tell he was thinking the same thing. How could they have trusted

Flash Buckley? Why didn't they know he was going to do something like this?

But when they finally unfurled the banner, Anna began to laugh. She laughed and laughed.

The banner said, in huge letters:

Go Chess Nuts!

'What are you laughing at?' Sophie said crossly.

Anna pointed, giggling, but Sophie frowned. 'There's nothing funny about it. You'd better calm down, because I'm not going to play someone who's hysterical.'

'Sorry,' said Anna.

'You will be,' Sophie said.

'Players, it is time to draw your colours,' Mr F said. 'Our invigilators, Dr P from Phoenix and Ms R from Condor South will be walking around to ensure that players are following the rules at all times. The game will begin at 12 p.m. sharp, and it will finish at exactly 1 p.m. At that time, if there has not been a clear win, the invigilators will determine the likely outcome. Their decision will be final. Spectators, I remind you that no noise is permitted during the game.'

Anna drew black, again. Sophie gave a superior smile.

'The games begin . . . now,' Mr F said. 'Good luck, everybody.'

Sophie opened by advancing her king's pawn, which Anna met with her own pawn. The pawns were fighting for control over the centre of the board; Anna considered an alternative move with her knight, but she was determined that she wouldn't let Sophie occupy the middle of the board without a struggle.

Then Sophie moved another pawn up next to the king's pawn to establish the King's Gambit. Sophie was offering up a pawn to Anna in exchange for control of the centre of the board. Now it was up to Anna – she could accept the gambit and take the pawn, or else she could hold her ground and fight.

Anna took a deep breath, and decided.

She held her ground.

Instead of taking the pawn, she moved her

dark-squared bishop up to the right side of the board to threaten Sophie's knight. But this gave Sophie the chance to take Anna's pawn for free.

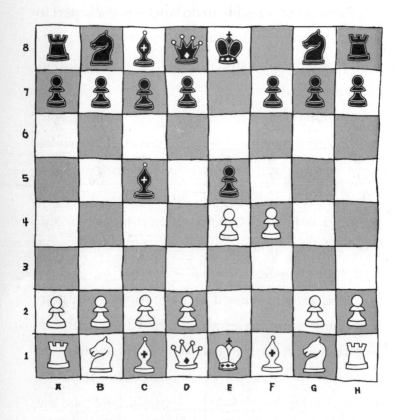

If Sophie studied the trap that Anna was trying to lay, she wouldn't take the pawn unless she was absolutely confident that she could counter Anna's attack. And Sophie looked confident all right. Her expression suggested she'd already won. Without waiting, she took Anna's pawn, and put it on the table with a crisp tap.

Now Anna was able to do what she did best – to attack. She moved her queen diagonally to the left-hand edge of the board.

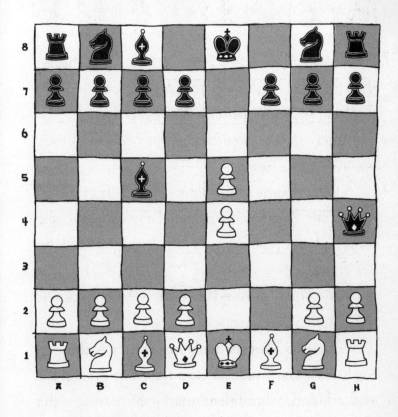

'Check,' Anna said.

Anna couldn't tell from Sophie's face whether she was surprised to have her king in check so quickly. But this time she took longer to move. Anna knew Sophie had one choice, and that was to move the knight's pawn up to threaten the queen. Otherwise, the next move would be checkmate, and Anna knew Sophie was too smart to let that happen.

Sophie moved her knight's pawn. And when she saw what was going to happen next, Sophie's forehead began to glisten with sweat.

Anna's queen swept across the board and took Sophie's king's pawn.

'Check,' Anna said, slightly louder this time.

Sophie took even longer to move. Again, she only had one choice – to block the check with her queen.

Now Anna delivered the blow that Sophie knew was coming. Anna paused.

'Come on,' Sophie said. 'Get it over with.'

Eventually, Anna slid her queen to the corner of the board, where she took Sophie's rook – the most powerful piece after the queen – for free.

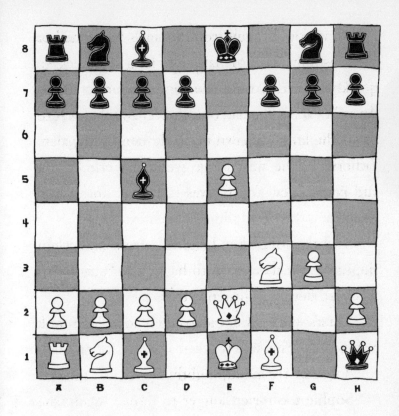

Sophie now focused her game on trying to capture Anna's queen. But Anna kept up her attack. Because Sophie had had to spend time blocking Anna's trap, she hadn't developed her pieces.

Anna had momentum in her favour, and she was determined to keep it. She moved out her knight, then her other bishop, and kept putting pressure on Sophie's side of the board. But Sophie came back with clever counters that made Anna have to work – and work hard.

One move. Another move. And another. Anna wasn't aware of the movements of the other players, or of Phoenix students watching her, or the time passing. There was nothing in the world except the chessboard and Sophie. Making one move, imagining the possibilities of the next.

And then the siren sounded. Anna hadn't got Sophie in checkmate yet, but she knew she wasn't far away from it.

She sat back and took a deep breath. Her chest ached, as if she'd barely taken a breath for an hour. She looked over at Sophie.

Sophie was furious.

'You were moving too slowly,' she said.

'I was not,' Anna said. 'I moved exactly how fast I needed, to have time to think.'

'Well, you should learn to think faster, then,' Sophie snapped. 'You were trying to distract me.'

'I was not!'

'Were so!'

'Girls!' Mr F said.

Anna remembered that she was in a competition. She looked up at the crowd, to see if Phoenix had won. But the crowd were all talking and shuffling around. Maybe they couldn't tell. Anna searched the other screens for information. Masha had won. Josh had lost. It looked as if Jackson had tied. That meant Anna needed to have won. But she didn't have enough time to analyse the remaining pieces before Mr F said, 'Ms R, Dr P, you will need to make a decision about this game.'

Anna's mother stood on one side of the board; Ms R stood on the other.

'I'm ahead in pieces,' Anna said.

'But my position is stronger,' Sophie said.

'Don't tell me what you think,' Anna's mother said. 'It is your move. Explain what you would do next.'

'It's obvious,' Sophie said. 'My rook is keeping her king to this side of the board. I would move my bishop here, and my pawn here. Anna would counter by preventing the check with her bishop, then I would take it and in two moves it's checkmate.'

'Sophie is right,' Ms R said. 'You started off well, Anna, but I can't see any other possibility now.'

Anna stared at the board. Was Sophie really right? If Sophie did check with her bishop, then of course she would have to defend it – and because she had been so intent on attacking, she had made the mistake of letting her own king get shunted into a corner – the most dangerous place for a king to be. Her heart turned to a stone in her chest. She had lost the chess championships for Phoenix, lost it as number one, which was even more shaming.

But then Anna looked more closely at the board. It was Anna's move. What if she moved her king now, out of the bishop's way, instead of continuing her attack? Anna saw each move, piece by piece, and blinked. Could that really be right?

'Come on,' Sophie said impatiently. 'You've lost. Condor South is the winner.'

'Silence!' snapped Anna's mother. 'She's concentrating.'

Sophie sulked. Anna ran through the moves again in her mind. Yes. She hadn't missed anything.

'Wait,' Anna said. 'I wouldn't have done what you say at all. It's tempting, but I wouldn't have. I would have moved my king to here – ' she pointed – 'and that changes everything.'

Sophie rolled her eyes. Then she looked at the board again. Anna saw her turn pale.

'Anna's right,' Anna's mother said. 'With that move, she has won.'

'I won?' Anna said.

Sophie looked as if she was about to faint from shock. Her jaw dangled as she examined the board frantically for other moves that she could make, but there were none. Finally, Sophie stood up and stuck out her hand barely long enough for Anna to shake it. 'Congratulations,' she said in a hard voice, and rushed off to the Condor South bus.

'I won,' Anna said, dazed. 'We won!'

A roar went up from the Phoenix crowd as Mr F announced, 'And the winner of the Chess Championships Grand Final for the A-team is . . . Phoenix!'

Anna looked at her mother. 'Thanks, Mum.'

'I didn't help you,' Anna's mother said. Then she added, 'You played a very good game of chess, Anna. The best you have ever played.'

And even though her mother didn't actually hug her, Anna felt as if she'd been hugged anyway.

And that was good enough for Anna.

Afterwards, the A-team had a party in C4.

Jackson's mother had baked a huge sponge cake, decorated with black-and-white checks made from chocolate, to look like a chessboard, and at either end were pieces and pawns made out of marzipan.

'Wow, Mum,' Jackson said.

'What a shame to eat it,' Masha said.

'I want the black queen,' said Anna. 'To keep, not to eat.' Then she added, 'But I want to eat some cake as well.'

Josh licked his lips and held out his plate.

'None of us could have won that endgame except you,' Jackson said, his mouth full of cake.

'Yes,' said Masha. 'You were amazing.'

'It was amazing,' Anna said. 'I really concentrated. I felt like the top of my head was lifting off.'

'Told you the running would help,' said Jackson.

'"Your body has to be in top condition",' Josh piped up. '"Your chess deteriorates as your body does." Who said that?'

Masha, Jackson and Anna looked at each other, and then said at once, 'Bobby Fischer.'

Josh gave a delighted shriek. Masha and Jackson laughed. Anna shook her head.

'Maybe he was right,' she mused. And then, in the middle of her musing, she was caught up in a big, squeezing bear hug.

'Dad!'

'My girl!' her father said, twirling her around. 'I'm so proud of you.'

'Dad,' she whispered. 'Put me down. I'm at school.'

'Sorry.' Anna's father smiled. 'I'm just so pleased. Hi, Jackson.'

'Hi, Mr P,' Jackson said.

Anna's father nodded to where Jackson's father was standing, talking to Anna's mother. From the gestures he made, Anna guessed they were talking about chess. 'I see your father's here. Good to see him up and about again.'

Anna had never seen Jackson grin so widely. 'Yeah. Me too.'

'Parents and chess players,' Mr F said, after clinking two spoons together to get everyone's attention, 'I'd like to thank you all for coming today. There will be a formal ceremony next week, but today I thank the parents for all their work in supporting your players. I'd especially like to thank Anna's mother, for being such an excellent invigilator.'

Everyone applauded. Anna's mother looked un-comfortable, but she nodded her acknowledgement.

'And I extend a special congratulations to the A-team for their outstanding efforts in beating Condor South today,' he said. 'This is especially significant, because Condor South came here expecting to win. No other school had beaten them, and they had thrashed us in the qualifiers. But we showed them what Phoenix is made of – Phoenix rose from the ashes and won!'

The chess players whooped and clapped; the parents whistled.

'Our players worked hard – in their bodies and their minds,' Mr F continued. 'They have proven the statement that "Chess is everything: art, science and sport." Can anyone tell me who said that?'

'Grandmaster Anatoly Karpov,' Jackson's father said.

'Very well done, Mr J,' Mr F said. 'I see where your son gets his chess knowledge from.'

Jackson's dad looked pleased. Jackson looked even more pleased. Even though he had tied, Jackson knew he'd played a good game against a good player. And his dad knew that, too.

'So please, everyone, enjoy the cake and the company. And chess players, when the festivities are over, you're welcome to go home early – you've earned it.'

Then Anna saw someone at the door.

'Flash?'

Jackson turned around when he heard the surprise in Anna's voice. Flash was walking towards Jackson. He was lugging the curled-up banner, which was half tucked under his arm, half dragging on the floor.

'I thought you might want this,' Flash said to Jackson.

'Oh,' Jackson said. 'Cool.'

'Seeing as you're like, king of the Chess Nuts now,' Flash added.

Jackson looked sharply at Flash, but Flash didn't have the evil glint in his eye that he used to have.

'Actually,' Flash said, 'the games weren't as boring as I thought they were going to be.'

Anna wanted to say, Wow, you must have grown a brain cell, but she thought that seeing as Flash wasn't being evil anymore, she shouldn't.

'I'll teach you some time if you want,' Jackson said.

Again, Anna wanted to say, Don't do that, you'll wear out the only brain cell he's got. Again, she bit her tongue. And again she thought about how she liked Flash better when he was his old evil self. There was something a bit strange about this new Flash.

Then Flash replied, 'Nah. It was still boring, just not as boring as, like, driving across Australia or something.'

Phew, Anna thought. He's still Flash all right.

'Here you go, then,' Flash said.

'Wait,' said Anna.

Flash and Jackson both raised their eyebrows at her.

'You can't give that to Jackson,' she said. 'He's only been called a chess nut for a few weeks. I've been called a chess nut for years.'

'So?' Jackson said.

'So, if anyone's going to get the banner, it should be me.'

'You didn't get yoghurt chucked in your bag,' Jackson said. 'Or a kick in the stomach at swimming training.'

'Sorry,' Flash said.

'No worries,' said Jackson.

'I think being publicly humiliated and teased since year four counts for more than a bit of yoghurt,' Anna pointed out.

'You never seemed to care,' Flash said.

'Well, that just goes to show what an ignoramus you really are,' Anna snapped.

'How many times do you want me to say sorry?' said Flash.

'A lot,' said Anna. 'Or, you could hand over the banner. Simple.'

'But Anna,' Jackson said. 'He came to give it to me.'

Jackson, Anna and Flash all frowned at each other. Anna huffed and Jackson sighed. Finally, Flash said, 'Wait. I have an idea.'

'What?' said Jackson.

'A race,' Flash said.

'Long distance?' asked Jackson.

'You'll win,' Anna said. 'Twice around the oval.'

'Three times,' Jackson said. 'It's got to be serious.'

'It's going to hurt,' said Anna. 'But why not?'

'And Flash,' Jackson said, 'you can be umpire.'

'Great,' grinned Flash. 'I like to see people in pain.'

Jackson was running.

This time, he wasn't running because he needed to clear his head, or to convince anyone to hold a public chess competition. He wasn't running because he wanted to win anything – although the banner would have looked pretty good in his room.

He was running because he was so happy he didn't know what to do with himself.

Anna was running too. She wanted the chess banner more than he did, and he didn't want to be seen to give something to Anna just because she wanted it. He was surprised at how fast Anna could run, just to try to keep up with him. She ran even faster the first time they went past Flash. Flash was sitting on one of the Kopper's logs, the banner resting next to him, and when he saw them approaching he gave them a big, loose, mocking round of applause.

'This was worth making a banner for,' he shouted. 'Run through the pain!'

'Shut up!' Anna growled. 'Just when I thought you'd forgotten how to be evil!'

Jackson kept running. It was just like Anna – even though she knew she'd never beat him, she decided she couldn't let him have the banner without a fight. She wouldn't let him have it easy, no way. The same thing that made her annoying was exactly the thing that made her a great chess player. Because that's what she'd proven she was, today – great.

Jackson was proud of the way he'd played, too. But the thing he felt proudest of was having his dad there.

Which is why he decided, even before they started running, that he would give the banner to Anna.

Because Jackson might have been running, but in everything that mattered, he'd already won.

ABOUT THE AUTHOR

Julia Lawrinson isn't a chess nut herself, but her daughter is one and her husband is another. In fact, Julia's husband might be a little like Mr F, and Julia's ferociously independent daughter might have partly inspired the character of Anna.

Julia is an award-winning writer. She has written many highly regarded young adult novels, including *Obsession*; *Skating the Edge*; *Bad Bad Thing*; *Suburban Freak Show*; *Bye, Beautiful* and *The Push*, the Aussie Chomp *Famous!* and one other novel for younger readers, *Loz and Al*.

You can find out more about Julia at www.julialawrinson.com.au